T0196926

ZOMBIE EVOLUTION

ZOMBIE EVOLUTION

BRENDA RENEE SEATON

ZOMBIE EVOLUTION

iUniverse books may be ordered through booksellers or by contacting:

iUniverse
1663 Liberty Drive
Bloomington, IN 47403
www.iuniverse.com
844-349-9409

Because of the dynamic nature of the Internet, any web addresses or links contained in this book may have changed since publication and may no longer be valid. The views expressed in this work are solely those of the author and do not necessarily reflect the views of the publisher, and the publisher hereby disclaims any responsibility for them.

Any people depicted in stock imagery provided by Getty Images are models, and such images are being used for illustrative purposes only. Certain stock imagery © Getty Images.

ISBN: 978-1-5320-8743-1 (sc)
ISBN: 978-1-5320-8742-4 (e)

Library of Congress Control Number: 2021910915

Print information available on the last page.

iUniverse rev. date: 05/25/2021

INTRODUCTION

Have you ever watched a movie involving zombies and thought, *Huh? Is this what zombies really are? Just dead carcasses that crave brains, have no heartbeat, and continue to function in a diminished capacity?* That's what we have been led to believe zombies are. Who hasn't watched *The Walking Dead* or *Night of the Living Dead*?

One might also describe a zombie as a soulless creature whose body parts are slowly decaying as maggots feast on it. Yuck! One would think life as a zombie was really a torturous and uncomfortable way to live, but wait—what has been planted in our minds is that zombies cannot feel, that they have no human emotions. That is the mind-set this book is meant to change.

What if I told you a zombie was really none of those things? Well, not all of those things anyway. You're laughing at me or getting ready to put down this book, but believe me, you're going to want to keep reading.

What if I told you a zombie was on the evolutionary

track humankind needed to get from point A to point B? I have your attention now, don't I? But you're still confused I bet. Let me explain. Humanity has always been on a path to self-destruction, but what if someone or something had a different plan for it?

Before I begin my story, which will change how you see the living dead and make you wonder about the person who created the concept of a zombie, do one thing—open your mind to the possibility that not all is as it seems. Clear your mind of any notion of what a zombie is and wonder about what it might be.

The day the black rain fell was the day humanity began on a new evolutionary path. Charles Darwin said, "One general law, leading to the advancement of all organic beings, namely, multiply, vary, let the strongest live and the weakest die."[1] You're wondering, *What does Darwin have to do with this story?* To answer that question and others that will enter your mind, let's go to the beginning.

The day like any other day was sunny and bright. Little did anyone suspect that clouds would form and the world would be changed forever.

---

[1] Charles Darwin, *On the Origin of Species*, 150th anniversary edition (New York, 2009).

Chapter 1

"Hey, Luce, whatcha doing?"

Lucy Johnson looked up from the book she was reading on the porch swing of a charming white house with a picket fence. "What's up, Sammy?"

Walking briskly up the walkway was Lucy's best friend, Samantha Crews. Samantha, or Sammy as her friends called her, had a bright smile and pigtails. She liked wearing overalls and tennis shoes. The two were as different as night and day. Lucy was a girl through and through; she always wore dresses and always had her chestnut hair styled as though she were in a beauty pageant.

"Just thought I'd see if you wanted to go to the fair in town today," Sammy said as she bounced up the stairs and plopped down on the swing next to Lucy.

Lucy looked at her best friend of thirteen years—they

had been friends since they were in diapers, and said, "Looks like rain today."

"What do you mean? The weatherman said it was going to be sunny and clear all day today. Not a cloud in the sky."

Lucy looked at her friend; her eyes changed from beautiful green to golden, and Sammy knew what this meant—Lucy was getting a feeling. Since they had been little, Lucy had an uncanny way of noticing or predicting when something bad was about to happen, and that would make her eyes change color. Sammy would never admit it, but that was the one thing about Lucy that scared her. "What's going on? What do you feel?"

"A feeling I've been getting for a while now. Something's coming. Not sure what, but I don't think anything will ever be the same again."

Sammy shivered at that statement.

Clouds suddenly began to form and thunder resonated. Sammy jumped, and Lucy quietly chewed on her tongue. They got off the swing, walked to the edge of the porch, and looked up at dark, angry, gloomy, and frightening clouds. Sammy stepped off the porch to get a better look at the clouds, but Lucy grabbed her hand and pulled her back on the porch.

"Ouch! Why'd you do that?"

"Sorry, but I don't think you need to be out there without cover."

Sammy looked at her best friend again and saw that her eyes had become an even darker hue of gold.

"Trust me, Sammy. We need to stay here today. Let's just watch some TV."

Sammy knew better than to question Lucy.

10:30 a.m. May 25, 2025, Haven Hospital

"Code blue—room twenty-three," came a voice over the intercom. Dr. Jessica Matthews raced through the corridor of Haven Hospital to the room where an elderly patient was in v-fib. A nurse brought in the crash cart.

"Charge to one hundred," Jessica said as she placed the paddles on the patient's chest. "Clear." The patient's body jumped as the current moved through her body. Jessica looked at the monitor and saw no sinus rhythm. "Charge to two hundred."

The nurse turned a knob on the cart and nodded at the doctor.

"Clear."

Again, the current coursed through the patient's body. The monitor still showed no signs of a normal sinus rhythm.

"Charge to four hundred. Clear."

The electricity caused the patient's body to jump again, but the sinus rhythm was still flat. "I'm calling it. Time of death, May 25, 2025, at 10:45 a.m. Nurse Prichard, where is the family?"

"In the waiting room down the hall, Doctor."

Doctor Matthews picked up the chart, made a note,

and calmly walked out the door. She took a deep breath and entered the waiting room. The family—three men of various ages and two women—had been crying. "I'm sorry" was all Jessica could get out before the women started wailing.

The men quickly moved to console them. The older gentleman, whose hair was slightly gray, said, "Thank you, Doctor. I'm sure you did all you could. My mother was seventy-seven."

Jessica pursed her lips and gave him a quick nod. She shook his hand. "I'll leave you to console your family. Your mother will be moved to the morgue. It will take a few minutes. You can make arrangements to have your mother transported to the funeral home."

"Thank you." He walked back to his family.

Dr. Matthews briskly walked out the door and ran into her husband, who was also a doctor. "Thomas, what are you doing in this wing?"

"Is that how you greet your loving husband of ten years?" He laughed at the startled look on her face.

"Sorry. I just had to deliver bad news to a family that their loved one just died."

"I know. I ran into Nurse Prichard. I came to find you. You usually get a little upset after you've seen a family."

"It's the one part of the job I don't like."

Thomas engulfed his wife in a hug. She laid her head on his chest and tried not to cry. She had always been a little emotional, and being six months pregnant, her emotions were tending to run a little higher than normal. Jessica moved out of his embrace.

Thomas laid a hand on her swollen belly. "How's the little one today?"

"Jumpy. She keeps kicking me in the ribs."

The smile on Thomas's face widened at his wife's need to refer to the child growing inside her as a she.

"What?" Jessica tried not to laugh at the amused look on her husband's face.

He stroked his beard. "You still insist we're having a girl?"

"Mother's intuition."

He laughed and winked at her. "Uh huh."

She playfully hit his chest, which caused him to laugh harder.

"You know all I want is a healthy, beautiful child, but having someone to play catch with or throw a football to would be awesome to say the least," he said.

She gave him a half smile and a quizzical look. "Are you saying a girl can't do those things?"

"True, true. A girl, especially ours, would be able to do those things and so much more."

She smiled radiantly at the serious look on his face. "Are you hungry?"

As they were heading down the corridor, the lights flickered, and they heard a loud thunder. The power went off, but the backup generator kicked in, giving the corridor a more menacing look. All the machines went crazy at once. Nurses and doctors were racing to each room to see if any damage had been done. Within a few minutes, the nurses and doctors had reassured all the patients that everything was okay. Hospital activity returned to normal.

After checking on their patients, Thomas and Jessica headed to the cafeteria and caught a TV news report as they passed a room: "Looks like it might rain today after all. Right now, it seems we're having an electrical storm, but nothing to worry about. We'll keep you updated on the weather conditions. Back to you, Dave."

1:00 p.m. May 25, 2025, a Home on Baker Street

"Tara, where's your brother?"

Tara looked up from her bed and took off her headphones. "I don't know. I'm not his keeper." She rolled her eyes before putting her headphones back on.

Janice Simpson shook her head at her daughter and walked away. She had been up since the crack of dawn cooking, cleaning, and doing laundry for her family of five—Bill, her husband of twenty years and their three children, twins Tara and Shawn and the youngest, Becky, who had just turned three. The twins were a handful at age sixteen.

She looked around their modest, three-bedroom home and sighed. Lately, it seemed to her that all her family needed her for was to take care of them. They barely uttered two words to her unless it was, "Mom, can you wash my uniform for football practice?" or "Honey, I'm hungry. What's for dinner?" Even Becky, who usually followed her around, didn't seem to be interested in what she was up to anymore.

Janice sat at the kitchen table, laid her head down, and closed her eyes. The front screen door slammed shut. "Shawn? Is that you?"

In walked Shawn, who was five-eight, blond, and slightly buff from playing football and lifting weights. "Yeah."

"Where the hell have you been?"

"At Jacob's. I spent the night, remember? It's written on the kitchen board on the fridge."

She looked at the refrigerator door and read the dry erase board on it. She took a deep breath. "So it is. I completely forgot to check there. But it also says you were going to be home hours ago. You have chores. It's your turn to take out the garbage and clean your filthy room. Didn't you hear the thunder?"

Shawn whined, "I just came home to change my clothes, get my football, and meet the guys at the park. The weatherman says it's nothing to worry about. Please, Mom."

"Maybe you should have come home on time."

Shawn bowed his head in defeat. "Please, I'll take out the garbage when I leave, and I'll clean my bedroom when I get home."

Janice took a deep breath. She sucked on her teeth. She knew that was the most she'd get out of him. If she made him stay home, she knew he'd pitch a fit and his room would be messier than it already was. "Fine, but I want a clean room tomorrow or you're grounded for a month."

"Thank you, thank you, thank you!" said Shawn as he leaned over and gave his mother a kiss on her cheek. She gave him a half smile and a halfhearted laugh, and he quickly bounded up the stairs. Within five minutes, he was back with his football. He grabbed the trash and almost ran into his father as he headed out the door.

"Hey! Watch where you're going, son!"

"Sorry, Dad. Gotta run." Shawn sprinted to the trash can by the curb, pitched the garbage in, and took off to the park.

Smiling, Bill kissed his wife. "Honey, I'm hungry. What's for lunch?"

Janice gave him an angry look and stomped out of the kitchen.

Bill was bewildered. "What? What did I say?"

1:45 p.m. May 25, 2025, Patton Park

"Hey, Shawn, what took you so long?"

"Sorry. Mom made me take out the garbage and promise to clean my room tomorrow."

"It's cool," said a boy who was about Shawn's age who was wearing blue Nike shorts and a blue jersey. There were ten boys altogether. "Let's divide up and play some football."

Two teams started playing touch football. Crackle went the thunder, and Shawn jumped. He shrugged it off. *Boom!* The thunder became louder and more sinister.

Jacob, Shawn's best friend and quarterback of the Mason High football team, jumped and lost his footing. "Ouch!" He stood but realized his ankle wouldn't support him.

Pete rushed over to Jacob's side. "Hey, guys, Jacob's hurt."

The others walked over to Jacob. "Let's get him to the bench under the tree."

Two boys carried Jacob to a bench. "What was that?"

"Sounded like thunder."

"Impossible! The weatherman said it would be sunny and clear all day." Lyle a friend of Shawn's looked confused.

Lightning flashed. Thunder boomed.

"Damn. I really wanted to play some football today. The last thing I want to do is spend my Saturday at home with my family cleaning my room," Shawn said.

"My ankle really hurts." Jacob grimaced as he rubbed his swollen ankle.

"Maybe we should take him to the ER at Haven."

The others nodded. Pete said, "I'll get my car from down the street." He rushed off.

The others talked about who would go with Jacob. "I'll go. That's a given," Shawn said. "He's my best friend."

"I'll go too," Lyle said.

The other boys told Shawn and Lyle to call them to let them know what happened at the ER. They departed, frustrated that the game had ended before it had even begun.

Pete pulled up in a four-door sedan; Shawn and Lyle helped Jacob into the back seat, and they headed for the ER.

3:00 p.m. May 25, 2025, Omega Observatory

Professor Robert Jenkins stood up in the bus and addressed his students. "We'll be spending the night at the Omega Observatory looking at the stars, planetary alignment, and any anomalies in the sky. Tomorrow, you'll write a ten-page paper about what you observed here tonight."

Some students groaned. Jenkins grabbed his backpack and sleeping bag and exited the bus, and the students followed him to an elongated white building with two round buildings attached at its ends. There were windows on each side. One round building was bigger and had a slit down the top. The glass doors opened, and out walked a man in a white lab coat followed by a young woman with auburn hair.

"Welcome," the man said. "I'm Dr. Jonathan Foster, and this is Dana, my daughter. I hope you'll learn the purpose of the observatory and come away with some knowledge of how the planets align as well as some insights about the fascinating subject of astronomy."

They saw lightning followed by thunder. "Follow me. You'll all have turns at the telescope. As this electrical storm continues, you might see some interesting things happening in the atmosphere."

They all grabbed their bags and followed Dr. Foster and Dana into the building.

The students walked into the room where the telescope was and were fascinated with its size. "This is called an optical telescope," Foster said. "It's used to monitor the atmosphere of Earth. It also monitors the stars as well as other objects floating in and around Earth's orbit. Who wants to go first?"

A young man wearing a light-gray T-shirt, blue jeans, and black flip-flops raised his hand. The scientist motioned him to come up and look into the telescope, and the young man ascended the stairs to the telescope. Foster extended his hand. "Hi. What's your name, young man?"

"Name's Danny."

"Nice to meet you, Danny. Look into the telescope and describe what you see."

It became strangely dark outside all of a sudden. The lightning cut through the darkness like a knife through butter. Thunder resonated through the building making everyone jump. Danny took a deep breath and once again looked through the telescope. "The clouds seem to be forming a barrier and are as dark as coal."

"Yeah, that seems to be the problem. No matter how we adjust the telescope, all we can see are the clouds and lightning. The machines are registering a change in the atmosphere. The oxygen levels are rising, and the nitrogen levels are falling. Normally, Earth's atmosphere is made up of 78 percent nitrogen, 21 percent oxygen, and 1 percent other elements."

Danny looked up from the telescope. "What happens if there's more oxygen in the air. I mean, don't we need to breathe more oxygen? Won't the pollution levels go down?"

"That's true. Warm-blooded animals would be able to run faster. Living creatures adapt quicker. However, there would be more fires because oxygen promotes combustion. Also, if the oxygen level increases to 100 percent, that could lead to things like hyperoxia and possibly oxygen poisoning."

"So humans can't breathe pure oxygen for a long time?"

"No," Foster said, "because humans and other warm-blooded animals need to expel carbon dioxide and other waste material, and that would be hard to do in a pure oxygen environment."

One by one, each student ascended the stairs and observed the sky through the telescope. After that, Foster suggested they adjourn to the cafeteria and put their gear in the rooms where they would sleep that night. "I'm hungry, and I bet you guys are too." Everyone nodded and followed the doctor out of the room.

4:00 p.m. May 25, 2025, Hampton Military Base outside the City Limits

A soldier exited the guard booth at the base gates and looked at the sky, wondering when the electrical storm would dissipate. He saw another soldier with an M-27 approach.

"Hey, soldier, Private Patterson reporting for duty at 1600 hours." Private Benjamin Patterson took his place at the post.

"Be careful. This weather isn't letting up like they said it would."

"It's just an electrical storm. It'll pass."

"All right, Benny boy, whatever you say."

The other soldier headed back to the compound and some much-needed rest. Ben looked at the sky and pondered the possibility of lightning striking the post. He chuckled at the notion and walked into the booth.

4:45 p.m. May 25, 2025, a Duplex on Stanton Way

Clicking off the television, Jessie Epson grabbed her purse and car keys. "Kylie, let's go! We have to pick Luke up from work before heading to the supermarket."

"I'm coming. Don't get your panties in a bunch." Kylie Milton walked downstairs and stuck her tongue out at her sister.

"You're assuming I'm wearing any," Jessie replied.

"Ewww! Too much info, sis."

Laughing at Kylie's expression, Jessie headed out the door. Kylie shook her head and stifled a laugh as she followed her sister. They piled into a black SUV and backed out of the driveway. They headed south to the freeway.

"Why do you need such a huge car, Jessie?"

Jessie shrugged and dug in her purse for a cigarette.

"Watch out!" Kylie yelled.

Jessie looked up just in time to swerve around a Mini Coop.

"Jesus Christ! What the hell's your problem?"

A shaken Jessie pulled over and took a deep breath.

"What's going on with you, Jessie?"

"I needed a cigarette."

"So bad that you can't pay attention to the road? You know I can't have that around me. I didn't bring my oxygen tank, just my inhaler. What's going on? Talk to me."

Jessie told her sister that she thought Luke was cheating on her.

"What gives you that idea?"

"He's been secretive lately—coming home late on the days he takes the car and hanging up the phone quickly when I walk into the room."

"Have you confronted him about it?"

Jessie looked at Kylie and started to cry. Kylie unbuckled her seat belt and pulled her sister into her arms.

5:00 p.m. May 25, 2025, an Office Building in the City

Luke heard a knock at the door. "Come in."

In walked a beautiful, sexy woman dressed in a tank top and blue jeans.

"Hi, gorgeous." Luke rose from his desk and drew her into his arms for a steaming-hot kiss. "I've missed you."

She smiled seductively and kissed him back. He caressed her ample bottom and nibbled on her neck; that caused her to squeal with delight.

The intercom buzzer sounded. "Mr. Epson, your wife's on line one."

"Thank you," he responded. "Shit. What time is it?" He looked at his watch and realized it was past five. "Damn. Jessie's picking me up. My car's in the shop for another week."

Lacy pouted.

"Sorry, sweetheart. I have to take this call."

Scrunching up her nose, Lacy grabbed her purse and turned to the door. Luke reached for her hand. "When is this game going to be over?" she asked. "You promised me you were leaving her. I'm tired of being number two."

"Baby, it's not that easy. I've been with Jessie since high school. I still care for her. It's not going to be easy letting her know I'm leaving her for another woman."

"Do you hear yourself? You're still thinking about her feelings. My feelings and our future are what you should be thinking about. I want to get married and have babies. You promised me this great future, and it's been six months. I'm tired of waiting. It's me or her. Choose now!"

Frustration showed on his face. "I have to make sure she's secure before I just leave her. She's depended on me for so long."

"You know what? Let me make it easy for you. Goodbye, Luke!" Lacy stormed out the door and slammed it behind her.

The buzzer went off again. "Mr. Epson, your wife is still holding."

"Thanks, Susan." Luke picked up the phone. "Hi, baby. Are you on your way?"

"Yeah. I'd have been there sooner but I was almost in an accident."

"What? Are you okay?" His eyes widened as she told him about her near miss, but after hearing what she had been doing, he erupted. "What the hell were you thinking of reaching for a cigarette while driving?"

Frustrated at his tone, Jessie handed her phone to her sister.

"Hey, Luke," Kylie said, "I'm going to drive the rest of the way. We should be there in about ten minutes."

"I'll meet you downstairs."

When Kylie pulled up to the curb in front of a twelve-story office building, Luke was waiting outside. Kylie got out, walked around to the passenger side, and got in the back. She gave Luke a look that said, *Leave it alone. Just be nice.*

Luke got into the driver's seat and leaned over to kiss his wife. A loud booming sound startled Kylie. "What was that?"

"Thunder. Haven't you been listening? It's been happening throughout the day."

"I guess I've been preoccupied. I've had my headphones on most of the day."

Rolling his eyes, Luke started the car and headed to the supermarket.

They pulled into the Scope Market's lot and got out. They heard another loud boom. "Looks like rain. Let's get just what we need and head home."

Lightning struck a phone line next to the supermarket causing sparks to fly and Luke, Jessie, and Kylie to flinch. "On second thought," he said, "let's go shopping tomorrow. I say we order in."

Kylie and Jessie agreed, and they raced back to the car and sped toward home. Rain began to fall fast and hard. The rain was black as coal and stuck to the windshield. Luke turned on the windshield wipers, but that didn't help much; the drops kept sticking.

They barely made it home in one piece. They pulled their coats over their heads and made a beeline for the door. Just as they got inside, the thunder became so loud that they had to cover their ears. The rain started falling in clumps and covering everything making visibility impossible. Kylie turned on the TV. A news reporter was standing in the rain reporting what was happening. "It seems to be raining tar. That's unusual and un—"

The reporter went from being coherent to snarling and attacking everyone around her. Kylie saw the alarmed look on Jessie's and Luke's faces. "What happened?"

The three watched the TV in stunned silence. The people on TV continued to change; they were becoming incoherent and pale. Their skin turned grayish white. They snarled and moaned. The cameraman must have jumped into his van because the footage looked as if it was being shot through a car window.

The silence in the room was broken by a violent cough. Luke and Jessie took their eyes off the TV. "Can't breathe …" Kylie collapsed on the floor, and Luke and Jesse were at her side in a flash.

"Where's her oxygen tank?" Luke asked frantically, but Jessie looked confused at his question. "Hello! Her oxygen tank she needs every day for her asthma!" Luke snapped his fingers in front of Jessie's face. Jessie shook her head to clear her thoughts and took off for Kylie's room.

She quickly returned with a small silver container with mask marked Oxygen. Luke took the tank and put the mask over Kylie's face, which had turned pale, almost transparent, as she struggled to breathe. He adjusted the nozzle to 10 percent above her usual intake, and she started breathing normally. They turned back to the TV and saw a reporter from the news studio addressing the situation.

"I don't know what just happened. It's uncanny. All

of a sudden we're being attacked by zombies. Is this real? Folks, we'll try to keep you updated."

They heard a banging noise coming from the TV. The news reporter turned to see where the noise was coming from. "What's going on?"

Luke, Jessie, and Kylie watched in horror as the studio door opened and snarling zombies invaded. People began running and screaming. The screen went black.

Chapter 2

Looking at the sky from the windshield of the car, Thomas turned to the guy sitting next to him. "Man, it's been a week since the rain fell. If you could call it rain."

Luke looked as well. "Yeah, I'm not really sure. I mean, it did stop falling like tar after about two hours and came down like rain, but it was still pitch black for two days."

Thomas parked on a street lined with houses. "We've been driving these streets every day since the rain stopped looking for survivors."

"Yeah. My wife and I were grateful you found us. Her kid sister was getting sick. We were wondering if trying to get to the hospital was viable."

Thomas shook his head knowingly and reached over the front seat for his gun and backpack. Luke reached behind for the shotgun on the back seat. "Have you ever wondered if shooting these zombies in the head was the right move?"

Thomas looks at Luke with a half smile and a quizzical look. "What do we know about zombies? One, they're essentially dead. Two, they attack anyone not like them. Three, when we shoot them in the head, they don't get up again, right?"

Luke bit his lip and nodded. "But we never really looked at one up close. Have we tried shooting them anywhere except the head?"

Thomas looked at Luke as if he were stupid. "Why would we risk our lives to experiment on some dead creatures whose sole purpose is to eat our brains?"

A voice comes over the walkie-talkie: "Team one, come in. Over."

Thomas pushed the button. "This is team one. Over."

"This is Shawn. Have you gone down Larimer Street yet?"

"No, that's not on our map today. Why?"

"That's where my family lives. I'm worried about them."

"Everyone at Haven Hospital has someone out there. We check a small grid every day. Hang in there. We'll get to that section of town soon. I'm sorry about your wait."

"It's cool, man. I was just wondering."

"Okay, but keep the channel open for emergencies."

"Will do." Thomas clicked his tongue. "Just do your job and keep us informed of any changes or danger at the hospital so we can get back if needed. Now radio silence, please. We're headed into dangerous territory."

"Copy that. Home base out."

Thomas hooked the walkie-talkie back on his belt and motioned for Luke to follow him to the first house on the block.

"Hey, Luce, I'm hungry."

"Shhh. Keep it down. We don't want to get them riled up again. They stopped banging on the basement door. We don't want them to know we're down here."

Sammy looked at Lucy and saw that her lips were quivering and that she was trying hard not to cry.

Lucy grabbed Sammy tightly. She brushed Sammy's reddish-brown hair out of her face. "It's okay, Sammy. Let's get some more canned fruit. Mom was always good about canning fruit and keeping other canned goods around in case of an emergency."

The girls quietly walked to a brown door in the back of the basement, which was damp and smelled like the earth after a good rain. The girls had been trapped down there for about a week. When the rain fell, the girls were inside. However, the rest of the family had been on the back patio enjoying the beautiful day. The rain fell without warning, and Lucy's mom and dad and older brother, Eric, had been caught in it. They had gotten inside, and for a while, everything seemed okay. But the next day, they had become violently ill and slowly began to show signs of becoming something other than human.

Around midnight the next day, Lucy woke Sammy up and motioned for her to be quiet and follow her to the basement. The banging on the basement door started shortly after that and continued for a while. The girls had been stuck in the basement ever since; they were afraid to find out if the family was still upstairs.

Lucy gently pushed the door open. In the room were jars of different sizes on shelves. She turned on the light. At first, it hurt the girls' eyes since they had been in the dark for a while. They blinked a couple of times, and Sammy smiled; she ran over to the jars with a sparkle in her eyes. She and Lucy grabbed some jars of peaches. "Oh my goodness, this is so good!" Sammy rolled her eyes and spun around to show how happy she was. Lucy let out a soft laugh, trying not to make too much noise. Sammy danced with her jar of peaches looking like a puppy doing a jump bounce for a treat. Lucy laughed so hard that peaches came out of her nose.

They heard a noise upstairs and became as quiet as mice. Sammy flicked the light off, and the girls hid behind a crate. The door to the basement swung open. Lucy put her hand over Sammy's mouth to stifle her scream. The basement became flooded with light. The girls looked up to see the figure step into the doorway. They screamed.

"Whoa! Turn down the sirens. Chill! We're not going to hurt you."

The girls saw someone else standing at the door.

"Hi. My name's Thomas, and my friend here is Luke."

"M-my n-name's Lucy. This is Sammy."

Thomas's smile reached his ears; it eased the tension. "How long have you girls been down here?"

"For almost a week. We came down here to hide from

the family. Sammy stays at my house a lot during the summer, and with the rain, I didn't want her to go home."

"There's no one up there now. It looks like the screen door was torn open. They must have left that way. Why don't we go upstairs to get you girls a change of clothes. We'll head back to home base."

Sammy gave Thomas a quizzical look. "Home base?"

Thomas smiled. "Haven Hospital, where most of the people who have not been infected live at the moment. We go out each day in teams of two to explore different areas. Sometimes we bring back people, sometimes we bring back food, and sometimes we come back with nothing."

"If you don't mind canned items, this room has lots of them," Lucy said. "My mom always canned fruits and made jams."

"Cool," Luke said. "I'll grab what will fit in our backpacks. Thomas will go with you upstairs."

Luke came upstairs about ten minutes later, and the girls had some clothes in pink backpacks with unicorns on them.

"Luke, you take the lead. The girls and I will follow."

Luke and Thomas put on their backpacks and waved the girls toward the door. They sprinted down the street to the car and piled in. "Home base, do you copy? Over."

"This is home base. Over."

"We're headed back with two packages in tow. Over."

"Copy that. We'll see you soon. Over."

"Copy that, team one. Out."

Thomas drove them to the hospital and pulled up to a wire gate surrounding a white, four-story building. Two men in camouflage gear were guarding the gate; each had an automatic shotgun slung over his shoulder. They unlocked the padlock and opened the gates; the car drove in, and they relocked the gate.

"I thought you said this was a hospital," Sammy said as she stared at the uniformed men and wondered what was going on. "This is a strange hospital if it needs guys with shotguns patrolling the area."

Lucy took her friend's hand as if to say it was okay.

Thomas parked; they grabbed their backpacks and got out. They walked to the entrance and were greeted by Jessica. Thomas said, "Young ladies, may I introduce my wife, Dr. Jessica Matthews."

Lucy and Sammy extended their hands and said in unison, "Pleased to meet you, ma'am."

"What polite girls," Jessica said, smiling as she shook their hands. "Okay girls, why don't you hand those adorable backpacks to Thomas and follow me to an exam room."

"Why do we need to do that?"

"You've been on your own for a week. We just need to make sure you're okay."

The girls looked skeptical, but they nodded and handed their backpacks to Thomas. They followed Jessica through the sliding doors.

"Hey, Jessica, have you seen my wife?" Luke asked.

"Yeah, Luke. She's with her sister."

"How's Kylie doing?"

"About the same I'm afraid. Her fever keeps spiking. I don't know what else we can do for her. It's wait and see."

"I'll drop my backpack in the kitchen and head to her room." He saluted her with two fingers and headed through the double doors. Jessica, Thomas, and the girls followed.

Luke walked down the hall and took the elevator to the second floor. He walked down the hall and pushed open a white door marked Room 201. Kylie was lying on a hospital bed with tubes attached to her. He heard her shallow breathing between the beeps of the oxygen machine. Her hospital gown was soaked with sweat. Her red hair was plastered to her scalp despite the fact that the room was cold from the oxygen machine. In the corner sleeping in a chair was Jessie. Kylie started coughing violently, and Jessie woke up, jumped out of her chair, and rushed to her sister's side. Kylie gasped and said, "Water."

Jessie filled the cup from the pitcher and helped her sister sit up by placing her hand on the small of Kylie's back. Kylie took the cup and drank slowly. She let out a deep breath and handed the cup to Luke. She threw up her hands and took a deep breath. "I'm okay."

Jessie pushed Kylie's hair off her forehead. "You sure?"

Kylie pushed Jessie's hands away. "Yeah!"

Jessie looked pained and hurt for a brief second.

"Sorry. I didn't mean to yell. I just hate being sick."

Trying not to let Kylie see her cry, Jessie hugged her sister. "It's alright. I understand."

"Hey, kiddo! Great to see you awake," Luke said prompting a grin from Kylie before she lay back on the bed. "We'll let you get some sleep."

Kylie nodded and closed her eyes.

Luke and Jessie slipped out the door. He put a hand on her folded arms. "You okay?"

Jessie teared up. Luke pulled her close and rested his chin on her head. She started shaking and crying. She pulled away from him and leaned on the wall in the hallway. "Sorry. I didn't mean to break down like that."

He tried to hug her again, but she yanked herself out of his embrace and walked farther down the hall. He ran his hands over his face and followed her. He put a hand on her shoulder. "Jessie, look at me please. What's going on?"

She looked at him with sad, green eyes. "I can't handle this anymore. I'm going out of my mind with grief."

Luke gave her a knowing look. "I know. I'm here."

"Are you, Luke? Really?" Jessie spat out the words as if they had a sour taste.

Luke let out an exasperated breath. "Baby, look. I know lately things between us haven't been that great. I've been distant lately, and for that I'm sorry. I love you. I just lost track of me and you. Please believe me when I say I'm here for you for now until the end of time."

She bit her lip. She took a deep breath. "Tell me the

truth. If you say you're here for me, I need the air cleared. Did you cheat on me? Is that over?"

He rubbed his temples and cleared his throat. "Yes and yes."

Jessie started to cry again. Luke pulled her into his arms. She pushed him away and started to hit his chest. He grabbed her and pulled her close. She stopped fighting and leaned into him as she cried.

"I'm sorry, sweetheart. You're my world. I screwed up. I'll never do that again."

Jessie looked up at him and swallowed. "I'll have to believe what you're saying, but know this, Luke. This is the only time I'll go through this. I'm willing to work this out. If you do this again, I'll kill you or at least maim that one thing you don't want to lose."

He laughed, but he knew she wasn't joking. He kissed her passionately to let her know he meant every word he had just said.

Sighing, Jessie leaned into his kiss. They broke apart and walked back into Kylie's room.

Chapter 3

Laughter came from the hallway close to Kylie's door. Four guys were hanging out having a good time. Two of the boys were in wheelchairs; one boy had a leg cast that went to his ankle.

"Okay, Jacob, are you ready to get your butt kicked?"

Laughing, Jacob said, "Pete, you're not going to win."

With a wink, Jacob pushed off and headed down the corridor. "Hey! That's cheating!" Pete said as he pushed off and tried to catch up with Jacob. He rounded a hallway corner and ran into Sammy and Lucy.

"Oww!" Sammy grabbed her arm as blood began to flow from the gash Pete's chair had just given her. Pete jumped out of his wheelchair and called for help.

Jessica and Thomas came running down the hall. "What happened?"

Pete looked up as he was applying pressure to Sammy's wound. "We were racing wheelchairs, and I came around the corner and ran into the girls. I didn't mean to hurt her."

Jessica took over from Pete and applied pressure to the wound. "It's okay. Let's get her on the stretcher." She and Thomas lifted Sammy onto the stretcher, where Jessica stitched her wound.

Lyle and Shawn came around the corner. "What's going on?"

"I ran into this girl as I was coming around the corner," Pete said.

Shawn looked at the gash in Sammy's arm. "Eww! Nasty gash you got there. It's going to leave a scar."

Jessica became angry and was about to say something when Lucy said something that put everyone on edge. "Something's happening! We need to hide *now!*"

"What do you mean?" Thomas asked. "We're safe here!"

Sammy looked into her friend's eyes and saw their color had changed. "She's right. We have to hide." She tried to jump off the gurney, but Jessica pushed her back down. "Stop moving or I'll mess up this stitch."

They heard static over the walkie and then a voice. "Can anyone hear me? Over."

"This is Thomas. Over."

"We've had a breach. I don't know how they got in, but there are zombies all over the hospital yard. Over."

They heard gunshots; the soldiers were firing their automatic rifles into the horde of zombies. Thomas turned to everyone. "Hide!"

Everyone quickly ran into the nearest room and shut the door.

"Jacob! He's still out there!" Pete yelled as he heard the sounds of a wheelchair out in the hall.

"Hey, guys, where'd you go?" Jacob called out as he looked behind him. He heard shuffling and moaning. He grabbed the wheels of his chair and started to make a run for it the best he could as he screamed for help.

The door on the far end opened. Luke raced out, grabbed the wheelchair's handles, and pushed him into the room. He slammed the door shut just as the zombies made it to the door. He and Jessie pushed anything they could in front of the door. They heard scratching on the other side. Kylie sat up in bed and made a very loud screeching sound. The scratching on the other side stopped. Luke peeked out of the small window on the door and saw the zombies shuffling away down the corridor.

Chapter 4

A voice came over the walkie: "They're leaving the building. Should we engage them?"

Another voice: "Negative. Let them leave and secure the perimeter. We need to understand how they got in and reinforce the area. Do you copy, Private?"

Private Patterson wiped his brow. "Yes Sergeant, I copy."

"Sweep the area. Make sure they're gone and then secure the perimeter. Does everyone copy?"

Several voices came over the walkie and acknowledged the order. Sergeant Rachel Johanson blew out the breath she was holding and got on the hospital intercom. "If anyone can hear me, the threat has left the building. We're securing the grounds. It's okay to come out of hiding."

Jessie and Luke pulled the barricade from the door. Jessie ran out into the corridor. "Jessica! Thomas! Anybody! Something's wrong with Kylie!"

Jessica and Thomas ran out of the room they had

been holed up in and were met by two nurses. In the room, Kylie was thrashing about as if she were having a seizure. "Get her on her side. Let's get some oxygen in here."

A nurse raced off for an oxygen canister and quickly returned with one. Jessica looked up. "I need everyone out of this room." Luke grabbed Jessie and tried to pull her out of the room, but she was as frightened as a child; her legs wouldn't move. Thomas spun her around to face him. "You need to move now! You're in the way. You cannot help her. Go!"

She snapped out of her daze and on shaky legs followed Luke out of the room. The door shut behind her.

It seems like hours, but it was actually only a few minutes until the door opened. The hospital personnel walked out. Jessica put her hand on her swollen belly and said to the others, "She's stable for now. Her fever spiked at a hundred and six. That caused the seizure. We were able to stabilize her. Her fever's receding. However, she's fallen into a coma. We'll continue to monitor her vitals. That's the best we can do for now."

Thomas put his arm around his wife causing her to flinch. He saw blood seeping from what appeared to be a scratch on her hand. He looked from it to her, and she gave him a weak smile. "It's okay. Kylie scratched me during her seizure. We know she's not a zombie. I just need to put some antiseptic on it. I'll be alright."

Thomas's smile didn't quite reach his ears. Jessica swayed, and Thomas and Luke reached out to catch her before she hit the floor. They eased her into a chair. She closed her eyes for a moment. When she opened them, she saw concerned faces staring at her. "I got dizzy. It's normal. After all, I'm pregnant. Final trimester. Things are getting harder to do. I overstimulated myself. I need some rest."

Thomas helped her up. "We'll bandage that hand, and you and I will go get some rest. There are more doctors and nurses in the building. If you need anything, just page one of them. Each nurses' station has a list of the doctors on that floor."

Thomas and Jessica walked down the corridor and disappeared around the corner. Lyle looked at the group. "I don't know about you, but I could eat."

They all nodded. They headed to the cafeteria.

Cafeteria workers were busy serving the people stranded at the hospital. Orderlies were pushing gray carts full of trays. The group grabbed trays and walked down the line. They found a table big enough for all of them. Lyle moved a chair aside so Jacob could fit in. They were silent as they ate.

Luke stretched and pushed his tray to the center of the table. "I have a question. Does everyone find it weird? That when Kylie screamed and screeched the zombies immediately left the hospital?" Jessie gave him a dirty look, but Luke shrugged as if to say, *What? It's a legitimate question.*

Pete said, "Wait. Was that her? I thought it was an owl or something. I mean, the noise was ear-piercing."

Luke clasped his hands together. "I'm just going to say it. These zombies are weird. Let's gather the facts. One, they aren't mangled. Most of them seem to be in good condition. Two, when people die, they stay dead. For instance, Mr. Brydle in room 223 died two days ago of appendicitis. He stayed dead. Aren't zombies supposed to be reanimated dead corpses? So why don't the dead come back to life? Something's not right here. I think we need to figure out what it is. I'm not comfortable going out each day and killing them if they aren't really dead."

Everyone pondered that. Lucy said, "Maybe everything we know about zombies isn't completely accurate. After all, we only know what we see on TV."

"Whoa," Shawn said. "Are you suggesting we capture a zombie and test this ridiculous theory of yours?"

Luke shrugged. "Why not? What harm would it do? As long as we're careful. We're not prisoners here. We're allowed to leave as long as we assume the risk once outside the gates. We sign out weapons and a van. Let's take a day to go find and test a zombie. We visit a pet store first and get a muzzle and maybe some twist ties somewhere so we can make sure we're safe from attack and test this supposedly ridiculous theory of mine."

Jacob said, "Sounds risky."

"Why don't we sleep on it? I don't have to go out looking for survivors tomorrow. Team two is up."

They all agreed that was a good idea.

Jacob patted his stomach. "I'm ready to go back to

racing down the corridor. I won, but I'll be fair and allow you losers to rechallenge me."

Pete laughed. "Dude, you cheated."

"I resemble that remark." Everyone laughed.

They took their trays to the dirty dishes table and left. Shawn, Pete, and Jacob headed to the corridor they had been racing in while Sammy and Lucy went to the lounge to watch a movie. Jessie and Luke headed to their room to catch some sleep.

Chapter 5

"Hey, Luce, what do you want to watch? We have *The Princess Bride*, *Galaxy Quest*, or my favorite, the Hobbit trilogy."

"That's what they put out for today? I vote to watch the Hobbit trilogy."

"That should occupy us for a while."

Sammy popped the first one into the DVD player, and the girls settled into leather reclining chairs. Before long, they were asleep and the movie had finished playing.

Lucy sat up as if she'd received an electric shock. She jumped out of her chair and shook Sammy, who opened her eyes, sat up, and groggily asked Lucy, "What?"

"I had a nightmare. Well, it felt more real than that. It was of a boy trapped behind a dumpster while the zombies shuffled down the alley. They didn't seem to notice him as they rooted through garbage like they were hungry. They were eating everything they could get their hands on. Maybe Luke's right. These zombies are weird.

They don't fit the usual criteria for what we classify as a zombie."

"Do you hear yourself? Criteria? Classify? Do you even know what those words mean?"

"I'm just thirteen, but I have an extensive vocabulary." Lucy rolled her eyes.

"Fine. Let's see if the hospital library has anything on zombies."

"This hospital has a library?"

"Yes, don't you remember a couple of years ago the mayor decided that patients needed more stimulation than just TV? All hospitals were required to add a library with a plethora of books for all ages."

"Plethora? Now who's using big words?"

The girls headed to the hospital library to do some research.

The elevator moaned and groaned as it descended to the basement. It came to a grinding halt. The doors slowly opened. They stepped out and let their eyes adjust to the poorly lit basement. "Which way?" Lucy asked.

Sammy looked at a board behind them and saw a sign pointing to the library. They held hands as they slowly made their way down the hall. They come to a wooden door marked Library. Pushing the door open, they had to let their eyes adjust again that time to bright light. A woman sitting at a desk was dressed like a typical librarian in a movie—hair in a bun, glasses on a chain around her neck, shirt with ruffles on the collar and sleeves. "Yes, may I help you?"

Sammy and Lucy approached her desk. "We need all the books you have on zombies please."

"Yes, may I help you?"

"Uh, we just told you what we needed."

"Yes, may I help you?"

"Jesus, lady, you need your hearing checked."

The girls were becoming frustrated, but Lucy took a closer look at the librarian and realized she was a machine. "Hey, Sammy, she's a mechanical librarian. We need to write our request on one of these note cards and feed it to her."

Sammy chuckled. She grabbed a note card, wrote down their request on it, and put it into the machine's mouth. Its eyes lit up, and the girls heard machine noises. "All books on zombies are in the fiction section labeled FIC-XYZ at the end of the right corridor. Thank you for your request. Please respect the library and return all books to their correct shelves when done." The machine shut down, and the girls walked to the section on zombies.

They indeed found several books on the living dead. "Hey, did you bring your notebook to write down what we find?" Lucy asked.

Sammy pulled the notebook out of her overalls that she always carried around so she could write down interesting facts whenever she and Lucy explored their surroundings. "Just because the world has changed doesn't mean I have to stop wanting to become a famous writer someday."

They started going through books for descriptions of zombies. "I think I found something," Lucy said. She laid her book down on the table so they could read it together, and Sammy took some notes. They found more information as they scanned more books. They learned that zombies had no feelings and killed without remorse.

"Sammy, let's look at what we know so far. When the zombies came to the hospital, they went after anyone they saw, right?"

"Yeah, but when Kylie screamed, they turned around and left."

"That doesn't seem like the zombies we're reading about, does it?" Sammy frowned in concentration.

"No, they should have migrated toward the sound, but instead, they fled as quickly as they could. They just walked out the door and past any human life they saw. They just wanted to get out of here. It was like they were told to leave and they went."

"Yeah, strange."

The girls continued searching through the books. Sammy started to read a passage from a book she had. Lucy looked up quizzically. "What does that have to do with zombies?"

"Think about it. We're trying to use the knowledge we're getting from these books of fiction to assess and determine how to deal with zombies, but do we have any real knowledge of what we're doing? Are we killing innocent people because of our ignorance? What real information do we have? Have we really looked at these zombies and explored all possibilities? This quote got me thinking. Maybe we need to look a little harder at the facts. We need to judge what we see against what we think we know. Illusion can cause so many problems. Do you remember when we liked magicians? We saw what they wanted us to see. Isn't that kind of what we're doing with these zombies?"

Lucy looked at Sammy with knowing eyes. "We need to finish gathering information and then present it to the others."

They went through all the zombie books they could and took more notes. Once their list was complete, they returned the books to the shelves and walked out past the mechanical librarian, which said, "Thank you for using the library. Have a nice day." They giggled as they pushed open the glass doors leading into the basement and to the elevator.

Chapter 6

It has been a week since the news had last been broadcast. The television showed only static. Janice looked at her husband, Bill. Her face was as white as a ghost. He pulled her in for a hug. The girls sat on the couch.

Tara could not believe what had happened. It had been a week, but she still saw the horror in her mind—nothing she could unsee.

Bill let go of his wife and looked at his family. "We need to make the attic a solid hiding place. The door is made of solid oak. We can hole up in there for days, maybe weeks. This may blow over soon. We just need to wait it out."

Janice looked at Bill and nodded. She wiped her tears and took a deep breath. She walked to the couch and wiped the tears off her daughters' faces. "Your father's right. I need you two to be brave. We need to get all the canned food from the kitchen to the attic. Blankets and pillows too. The camping gear in the garage. We'll have a campout in the attic. It'll be fun." She smiled trying to soothe their fears. "The attic can be our safe haven."

Bill put a hand on his wife's shoulder and looked at his daughters. "Okay, my angels, it's time to get to work."

Becky looked at her father. "What about Shawny?"

He picked up Becky and cradled her. "I don't know, little one. We just need to hope and pray he's safe. He'll find his way home. I have faith that your brother is somewhere. He's strong, and if God's willing, we'll be together again."

"God doesn't give you more than you can handle, right, Daddy?"

He hugged her. "That's right, my angel. Never forget during these trying times that we must always look to God for answers."

They moved all their supplies up to the attic, and Bill and Janice took turns guarding the house and looking out windows for any sign of Shawn. They were showing signs of fatigue. Janice went to bed when Bill took over. He rubbed his eyes and stifled a yawn. He sat in the rocking chair facing the back door with his rifle in his lap. His head dropped, and he nodded off.

Two hours later, the front door knob began to rattle. Janice sat up in bed and grabbed the rifle next to the bed. She ran to the front door and saw it was still bolted. She looked out the window and saw a zombie, which headed to the window and began to beat on the glass. Other zombies joined her. Bill came running toward the noise. "What was that?"

"Zombies! They're trying to get into the house!"

Bill looked out the window. "Get the girls to the attic. I'll try to hold them off." Janice hightailed it to the girls' room. "Tara! Becky! Wake up! Get up to the attic!"

Tara asked, "What's going on?"

"There's danger. I need you and Becky to get up and secure yourselves in the attic. Be quiet and have your rifle ready just in case."

"In case of what?"

"Tara, please. Don't ask any questions. Just go quickly and lock yourself in there."

Tara threw back her covers and grabbed Becky. Janice headed back to the living room as Tara and Becky headed to the attic. Tara locked the door. She and Becky huddled in the corner.

Janice and Bill tried to hold off the zombies. The bay window, close to the ground, broke, and zombies climbed in. Bill and Janice shot at them and hit the first few, but they needed to reload. They backed up toward their bedroom. Bill tried to shoot a zombie who had grabbed his arm. The rifle tilted up. The shot went into the ceiling. Tara stifled a cry. The zombie bit Bill's neck. He pushed against the zombie's head knocking him to the ground. He shot him in the head, and brain matter and blood splattered the walls and floor.

"Bill! Are you okay?"

Bill put his hand on his neck and came away with blood. Janice felt a jerk on her hand and noticed a scratch. They looked at each other and retreated to their bedroom. They blocked off the door as zombies tried to get in. Bill went to the nightstand and retrieved letters he had written the previous night. He found the one he wanted and put it on the nightstand. He removed the handgun from the nightstand. Janice lay on the bed. He lay down next to her. "I love you," she said.

"I love you too," he said. He pointed at her temple and fired. He turned the gun on himself and pulled the trigger. The gun fell to the floor.

Chapter 7

Bryce opened the door slowly. What he saw made his stomach turn—blood and guts everywhere. He motioned for his partner to follow. Paul pushed open the door and instantly stepped on something squishy. "Yuck." Paul lifted up his combat boots and wiped it on a chair by the door. Bryce put his finger to his mouth. "Shhh."

Paul said, "Sorry."

Bryce motioned Paul forward again. "Watch your step. It's a slaughterhouse in here."

They cautiously stepped around the blood and guts, walked down the hall, and approached a closed door. Bryce opened the door slowly. He almost lost the contents of his stomach at the sight. There were no zombies in the room, just two people lying on the bed each with a bullet wound to the head. A gun was lying on the floor. They saw a note on the nightstand. He entered the room trying not to gag. He chuckled to himself. He could shoot a zombie, but dead humans made him sick. "Get it together, Bryce," he whispered to himself.

Paul walked in and saw the bodies on the bed. "Oh man. What happened?"

"Not sure, but there's a note on the nightstand. Can you get it? I need to get out of here before I get sick."

He pushed past Paul. Outside of the room, he drew a deep breath. Paul followed with the note in hand. "You all right?"

"Yeah, I'm okay. What does the note say?"

Paul skimmed the note. "Basically, it says if you're reading this, we're dead. Wait. It says their daughters are in the attic."

"One way to find out."

Bryce and Paul searched the house for the stairway up.

"Tara, what's that noise?"

Tara pulled her sister close and pushed her bangs off her forehead. "I don't know. Shhh. We just need to be quiet."

"I'm scared."

"I know."

Tara got up from her hiding place and grabbed the rifle. She checked the chamber to make sure it was loaded as her father had taught her and crept over to the door.

"Sissy! Don't leave me!" Becky said.

"It's okay, Scooby Doo. I'm not going anywhere."

Becky smiled at the mention of her nickname and stifled a cry.

They heard banging on the attic door. Tara raised her rifle. The door burst open and Tara prepared to fire.

Bryce held up his hands in surrender. "Whoa! Hold on! We're here to rescue you. Please come with us. We'll get you to safety."

Tara lowered her rifle and began to cry. Becky came out of hiding and ran to her sister, who engulfed her in a hug.

"Okay, young ladies, we need to go. It'll be dark soon, and the zombies will attack."

Tara nodded and took Becky's hand. They followed Bryce and Paul downstairs. Paul got ahead of them and quickly pulled the bedroom door closed. They ushered the girls out of the house and into the van.

"Where are our parents?" Tara asked.

Paul lied. "I don't know. We didn't see them. Just get in. We'll look for them, but we need to get you to safety first."

The girls piled into the van, and Bryce drove off. Paul got on his walkie. "Home base, do you copy?"

"This is home base. Over."

"This is team two. We're returning with two packages in tow."

"Copy that, team two. See you when you get here. Home base out."

"Where are we going?" Tara asked.

"Haven Hospital. We'll be there soon."

Tara pulled her sister close and looked out the

window. She hoped they hadn't made a mistake trusting these people.

Tara did not realize she had fallen asleep until Paul opened the door and shook her gently. "Here we are here."

Tara woke Becky. They got out of the van. Tara looked around and guessed they were in an underground parking garage. They exited the garage. The sun was blinding. They all walked to the entrance.

Chapter 8

F our people pushed through the glass doors into the hospital and approached the reception desk. "Hey, Nancy, team two returning with packages in tow."

"Hey, Bryce. Who are these packages?"

Bryce looked at the girls and gestured for them to respond. Tara held her little sister's hand and approached the desk.

"Now sweetie, no need to be afraid. I don't bite," the nurse said.

Tara gave the nurse a timid smile. Becky gave the nurse a huge smile. "My name's Becky I'm three."

"Well hello, Becky I'm three. That's an unusual name."

Becky's smile got bigger. "No, silly. My name's Becky. And I'm three years old." Becky put a hand over her mouth to stifle a laugh as Nancy and Bryce chuckled.

Nancy looked at Tara, who seemed a little scared. Tara gulped and licked her lips. "My name is Tara Simpson, and this is my sister, Becky."

Bryce frowned in concentration. "Don't we have someone here by the last name of Simpson?"

Nancy's eyes lit up as if she'd just gotten the biggest idea ever. "Yes we do." She got on the walkie and paged Shawn to the front as well as the doctor on duty. Shawn answered over the walkie "Hey, Nance. Whatcha need? It's not my shift at the home base."

"We have two new members."

"Okay." Shawn sounded annoyed "I'm not the welcoming committee."

"Just get to the front and stop giving me grief. You'd think I was asking you to clean your room."

"Fine. I'm on my way."

Dr. Joseph Crane came around the corner and greeted Nancy, Bryce, and Philip. He looked at Tara and Becky. "I see we have new members to this ever growing family. Hi, girls. I'm Dr. Joseph Crane. I'll be looking you over and making sure you're okay."

Shawn came around the corner looking very annoyed. He didn't spot the girls right away.

"Shawney!" Becky yelled and ran straight at him. It took him a few seconds to register who the blob running his way was, but then he bent down and opened his arms. Becky ran right into them knocking him down and causing him to lose his breath. He stood up, and Becky wrapped all four of her limbs around him. He then noticed Tara standing at the desk in tears. He shifted Becky to his hip and walked to Tara to engulf her in a much-needed hug. He kissed her cheek. "I'm so happy to see you guys! I was afraid I'd never see you again. Where's Mom and Dad?"

Tara burst into tears and shook her head. Shawn's hug became tighter. Nancy brought Tara a paper cup of water. "Here, honey. Drink this. We don't need you to hyperventilate." Tara nodded at Nancy in thanks and drank it.

She looked at her brother. "I don't know. When the zombies started attacking our house, Mom made us hide in the attic. We heard a lot of noise—Mom and Dad were shouting. Then we heard gunshots. I had to keep Becky quiet. We stayed hidden until Bryce and Phillip showed up."

Shawn looked at Bryce and Paul, and Bryce looked at Shawn with a sad expression. "Sorry, kid. When we got there, your parents were in their bed holding each other. They had bullet wounds in their heads. It was a murder-suicide. They left a note. They'd been bitten. They wanted to make sure they didn't turn and attack your sisters."

Paul took over the story. "We didn't want your sisters to see them."

Shawn, Tara, and Becky cried for a few minutes. Shawn put Becky down and extended his hands to Bryce and Paul. "Thank you." They shook hands.

Bryce and Paul turned in their guns. "It's been a long day. We need to eat, shower, and sleep." Bryce and Paul gave everyone a two-fingered salute and headed to the cafeteria.

Dr. Crane said, "I need to check the girls out. Then they can eat and shower and hopefully get some sleep."

Tara looked down at her torn and ragged clothing.

"Don't worry," he said. "I'm sure we have a change of clothes in our clothing store. Whenever the teams go out, they try to bring back clothing of different sizes so everyone can have clean clothes. Follow me."

Shawn, Tara, and Becky followed Dr. Crane down the hall and around the corner.

Chapter 9

Shawn waited outside the shower stalls as his sisters showered and changed. The door opened, and they walked out. Alarms sounded throughout the hospital causing Becky to jump. Hospital personnel raced down the hall to the elevator.

Tara looked at Shawn. "What's going on?"

"It's coming from Kylie's room. She must be in distress again. Come on. We can see if Jessie or Luke needs reassurance."

They headed to the elevator. Shawn pushed the button for the second floor. When the doors opened there, they stepped out and Shawn led them to the waiting room. Luke was looking out the glass door at the room across the hall.

Shawn saw Jessie sitting on the edge of her seat biting her nails. "Hey, guys. What's going on now?" he asked her.

Luke answered him without turning around. "She had another seizure. Thomas and Jessica are in there with her." Luke turned and noticed Shawn's two companions. "Who are these lovely ladies?"

"These are my sisters, Tara and Becky."

The door to Kylie's room opened. Thomas came out followed by a very pale Jessica. Luke and the others met them in the hallway. Thomas answered the question on everyone's mind. "She's stable again. Her fever spiked to a hundred and six again. This seems to happen once a day. She's still in a coma. We'll keep monitoring her of course, but I'm worried that if she doesn't wake up soon, there might be some brain damage."

Jessie started to wail. Luke rushed to her, caught her, and lowered her to the floor. Her crying turned into hiccups. "She's hyperventilating," Jessie said.

Thomas sat on the floor next to Jessie. "You need to take deep breaths. I need you to calm down. Otherwise, you'll be in a bed beside your sister. That won't do her any good."

Jessie breathed deeply several times and got herself under control.

"There you—" He didn't finish his sentence before Jessica grabbed her belly as water spilled out of her. "Thomas! I think I'm in labor."

He rushed to his wife's side. "Call for help. I need to get her to an empty room." He half-carried her down the hall as she started having contractions.

Shortly after that, Dr. Crane walked calmly into the room. Jessica was hooked up to a fetal monitor and another that measured her contractions. He read the paper coming out of the machine. "Looks like the baby's not in any stress and the contractions are coming at regular intervals."

"But Doctor, I'm only seven months along. It's too early. I shouldn't be having her for another two months."

"I understand you're scared, but the last time you had an ultrasound, she was fully developed. She might be born small, but I don't think there'll be anything to worry about."

A contraction hit Jessica, and Thomas helped her breathe through the pain.

"Contractions are coming two minutes apart." The doctor moved to the foot of the bed and lifted the sheet. "You seem fully dilated."

The doctor and nurses got ready to bring Jessica's baby into the world.

"Okay, Jessica, when I tell you to push, you push." The doctor sat on a roller chair. "Push." Jessica started pushing during one contraction and then another.

"Okay, the head's crowning. Give me another push." Jessica pushed.

"One more push to clear the shoulders."

Jessica pushed really hard. The newborn started wailing. "Congratulations! It's a girl!"

Jessica and Thomas smiled as the nurse laid the baby in Jessica's waiting arms. "She's beautiful."

Jessica leaned her head against the pillow, and Thomas kissed her forehead.

"What's her name?" the nurse asked.

In unison, Jessica and Thomas said, "Trisha Mae Matthews."

"Nice to meet you, Trisha Mae Matthews. I need to take you now. When you're cleaned up, I'll bring you back to Mommy and Daddy."

"Bye, Trisha. We'll see you in a little while."

The nurse walked out the door holding the little pink bundle of joy.

Chapter 10

J essica sat up quickly and reached for her stomach, which was flat. She panicked for a minute before she realized she'd given birth a few hours earlier. She saw Thomas sleeping in the hospital chair with his head at a weird angle. She knew he would have a stiff neck if he didn't wake up soon. "Thomas? Thomas?"

He woke up and snorted. He shook his head to clear his mind, looked at Jessica, and smiled a very sleepy smile. "Hi, my love. Did you get some sleep?"

"I did. Where's the baby?"

Thomas got up and hit the intercom button. "Nurse, can you bring in our baby? We'd like to see her." Silence. "Nurse? Did you hear me?"

"Yes, Doctor."

Dr. Crane walked in looking very serious; that set off alarm bells in Jessica's mind. "Where's my baby? What happened?"

"I don't want to alarm you, but Trisha's in the neonatal ICU."

Thomas sat on the edge of the hospital bed and gave the doctor an angry look. "Why weren't we informed?"

"It happened about twenty minutes after the nurse took her to be cleaned and dressed. You were so tired and had fallen asleep immediately. I didn't want to frighten you or cause panic if it was nothing. She spiked a high fever and had to be put on oxygen. She's resting now, but we can't seem to remove her oxygen. It seems she requires a higher dose than most humans do. Her symptoms mimic those of Kylie Milton."

Jessica's hand covered her mouth to stifle a cry. Thomas tried to hug her, but she pulled away and shook her head. "Kylie's no zombie! There shouldn't have been any contamination."

Dr. Crane looked at his chart. "Did something happen when you were caring for Kylie? Did she cough on you or bleed on you?"

Jessica shook her head. "Wait. She did scratch me when she was experiencing a high fever and seizing."

Dr. Crane pondered that for a moment. "She might have infected you with something that entered your womb and infected the baby. It might also explain why you went into labor early. The baby couldn't get enough oxygen and needed to be born. Were you light-headed at all after the scratch?"

"Yes, a few minutes after, but I just chalked it up to being pregnant and overstimulating myself."

"Until we can diagnose what ailment Kylie and Trisha have, we'll have to supply them with the oxygen they need, about 29 percent higher than normal human needs."

"So that's about 50 percent oxygen."

Dr. Crane nodded.

"Can we see her?" she asked.

"Yes. I'll get a wheelchair for you."

"Thank you, Doctor."

Dr. Crane left, and a few minutes later, an orderly rolled in a wheelchair. Thomas helped Jessica into it, and they headed to the NICU.

Jessica and Thomas entered a sterile environment. Trisha was on a small bed surrounded by hard plastic with holes that allowed the doctors and nurses access to her and let the parents comfort her.

Thomas pushed Jessica over to the incubator. Jessica put her hands on the plastic covering and started crying. "It's all my fault!"

Thomas took her wet face in his hands. "No, sweetheart, it isn't. It's just the nature of the beast. Look at her. Other than the need for oxygen, she's okay. We'll figure this out."

Jessica drew a ragged breath and reached through the plastic to touch and comfort her child. Trisha wiggled like a normal baby even though she has an oxygen tube attached to her nose.

A nurse came in and smiled. "The doctor says all her vitals are fine. We can remove her from the incubator and place her in a crib. She needs just the oxygen. You can hold her if you like."

Jessica smiled and wiped her eyes. "Yes, please."

She wiped her hands with a wet wipe Thomas had fetched from a table nearby. The nurse lifted off the hard plastic covering and set it aside. She very gently picked up Trisha to avoid dislodging her oxygen tube. The nurse placed the baby in Jessica's arms. Jessica cradled her and kissed her forehead. "Oh my sweet angel."

Trisha became fussy. "She's hungry. Can you hold her for a second? I need to get ready to feed her." Thomas took Trisha from Jessica; she adjusted her gown so she could feed the baby. Thomas handed Trisha back to Jessica, and Trisha latched right on and began to feed. Jessica covered her with a blanket and leaned back sighing with relief.

Chapter 11

A young boy about ten sat huddled with his mother and sister in a dark, damp warehouse. They had one blanket between them. "Mom, I'm hungry."

His mother swept his brown hair out of his face. "I know, baby. We'll have to go out. I need for you and your sister to stay close. I need both of you to run the minute there's any danger."

Sophie stood and put her dirty blond hair in a bun. Jamie picked up a crowbar and a bat. She handed the bat to Sophie. "Tyler, stay close to your sister. Don't leave her side."

"Why can't I have a weapon?"

"Because you're too little. Your sister and I are better equipped to handle the threat."

Tyler pouted but agreed to stay by his sister's side. He didn't understand that because his sister was only two years older. He took Sophie's hand.

The small family creeped out of the warehouse using the shadows as cover. Jamie slowly opened the door and looked around to make sure the coast was clear. She motioned for the children to follow. They made their way outside. They heard movement and saw the chaos that had occurred. The blood and guts of what appeared to be a small animal were smeared on the parking lot.

"What's that?" Tyler asked.

"I don't know. We need to keep moving."

They walked across the parking lot and headed to the nearest row of houses. Jamie poked her head in the window of one and saw no zombies inside. She tried the door, but it was locked. She checked the window and got it to lift enough for a small child to get through. "Tyler, come here." She lifted him up and slid him through the opening. "Don't be afraid, son. Just open the door." Tyler nodded and walked to the door. He opened it allowing his mother and sister to enter. "We need to find any food that's edible quickly. We need to get back before nightfall. The zombies will emerge soon."

They walked into the kitchen to look for food. None of them realized the front door hadn't closed all the way. They rummaged through cabinet doors. "We need something to put this food in." Sophie discovered a box of trash bags. Jamie took one and gave her children some. They filled them with canned goods. They were making so much noise in their hurry that they didn't hear the front door open. They didn't notice the zombies until it was too late.

Tyler turned around. "Mom! Look!"

Jamie followed Tyler's gaze. "Drop everything and run!"

Tyler grabbed the back door handle and tried to open it. Jamie and Sophie battled the zombies with their weapons. Jamie took her eyes of the zombies for a second to check on Tyler and a zombie grabbed her arm. As she was pulling free, the zombie's nails dug into her flesh leaving a gash that bled heavily. She bashed the zombie's head in with the crowbar and snatched up a hand towel next to the sink to bind her wounds.

Tyler was still struggling with the door; his hands were slippery from sweat. Sophie yelled for him to hurry. She swung the bat at a zombie trying to bite her. She backed up to the door trying not to take her eyes off the zombie, which had rotten teeth. She quickly yanked the door open. The zombie managed to bite her arm and take out a chunk of flesh. Jamie smashed its head in, and the zombie fell to the floor. They ran out and hightailed it back to the warehouse. Inside, they slammed the door shut.

Jamie and Sophie fell to the floor. Their breathing was becoming labored and their skin was turning gray. Jamie looked at her son and said, "Run!" Tyler took a deep breath and quickly backed up to the door. Jamie and Sophie got up and advanced on Tyler.

He turned and raced out the door. He did not see his mom or sister follow. He did not hear them try to say his name. His heart was all he could hear. It was beating so loud. It felt like it was going to jump out of his chest. He found the first alley he could and crawled behind a dumpster. He hid in the shadows as zombies roamed around. Tyler closed his eyes and covered his ears.

Chapter 12

Lucy knocked on a door marked 202. The door opened. Luke licked his lips and blinked a few times before asking, "Hey. What's up?"

Lucy bit her lip. "You remember yesterday in the cafeteria? You wanted to test your theory on the zombies?"

Giving her a half-quizzical and half-mad look, Luke nodded.

Lucy gulped. "Sammy and I went to the library in the basement and did some research on zombies."

She handed him a green spiral notebook. He opened it and read a list of what zombies were according to the books and a list of what was known about them from sight. Lucy put her hands in the pockets of her pink sweater and rocked back and forth on her black dress shoes as Luke read.

His face showed signs of approval; he nodded as he read. "Thanks, Lucy. This'll come in handy. It's about seven. My wife and I need a few more hours of sleep.

How about we meet in the cafeteria in two hours? Do you remember where everyone's room is?" Lucy nodded. Luke scratched his face. "Hmm. Need to shave too. Okay, slip notes under everyone's door and tell them to get to our table in the cafeteria at nine. See you then." He shut the door and crawled back into bed with Jessie. She snuggled back into his embrace.

"Who was at the door?"

"Lucy. We have a meeting at nine for breakfast."

"What time is it?"

"Just seven." He drew her closer and kissed her neck. She smiled a sleepy smile and turned to him. He pulled her in for a deeper kiss. "We may be a little late."

She chuckled and kissed him, biting his bottom lip. "Yeah, we're going to be late."

"Where are they?" Lyle asked as he looked at his ancient wristwatch.

"Does that thing really keep accurate time?" Pete asked. "It's like a hundred years old. Nobody wears a wristwatch anymore."

"It keeps perfect time. It was my grandfather's."

Jessie and Luke showed up holding hands. They quickly went through the line for breakfast and joined the others.

"What took you so long?" Lyle asked.

Luke was beaming as he shoveled food into his mouth. Shawn jabbed Lyle in the side. "Dude, if you haven't figured that out, you're an idiot."

Lyle turned deep red. He looked away to get it under

control. Tara giggled at the stunned look on Lyle's face. Luke pushes his tray to the middle and pulls out the little green notebook Lucy had given him that morning. Sammy checked the pockets of her purple overalls. "Hey! That's my notebook!"

Luke opened it. "The girls gathered a list of what a zombie is according to the books in the hospital library. According to it, zombies are essentially dead. They have no heartbeat, no feelings. They crave brains, have diminished brain capacity, and kill or turn every living thing. Okay, now for what we've observed. They do seem to have diminished brain capacity, and they ran when Kaylie screamed. The dead stay dead. Huh. Not much."

"I have a few questions. Are they essentially alive? What's causing their diminished capacity? If the dead stay dead, what keeps the others going?" Luke looked around the table. "This will be a dangerous mission. We have to be careful not to get scratched, bitten, or eaten. I think only a few of us should go. Shawn, Lyle, Pete, and I."

Anger showed on Jesse's face "I'm going too."

Luke pretended not to notice her defiant look that if it could kill, he'd be dead. "I think you should stay here. I mean, what if Kylie wakes up?"

Tara raised her hand as if she were in school. Luke gave her a look. "Yes?"

"I'll watch Kylie."

Jessie gave Tara a hug. "It's settled then. I'm going.

Whatever's happening is affecting my sister, and I need to be involved."

"Fine, you win," Luke said.

Smiling like a giddy schoolgirl, Jessie kissed Luke's cheek. "I know."

Everyone laughed at that.

They saw Thomas leaning against a column. "If you insist on doing this, you'll need a doctor. Besides, it'll be easier getting past patrols with me if we pretend to be looking for food and supplies. They won't question that." Everyone nodded.

"Damn it! I wish my ankle wasn't broken so I could go," Jacob said with a sigh.

Luke said, "We'll want to communicate with you guys, so why don't you be our home base? We'll change the frequency on the walkies and communicate with each other. You can be the go-between."

Jacob seemed content with that. They agreed to stay together so communications would be less noticeable.

Lucy said, "I need you to do me a favor please."

Luke looked at Lucy and saw a golden hue in her eyes. "What's that?"

"I had this dream yesterday about a boy trapped behind a dumpster in an alley off High Street. I know it might have just been a dream, but something tells me that it was real and that he needs help. Would you please go down the alley and check it out?"

"High Street?" Luke asked. "I know where that is.

It's not far from here. We just have to turn left when we leave here."

Lucy's eyes began to fade to normal. She breathed a sigh of relief.

"Okay guys, let's go."

Chapter 13

Thomas walked to the reception desk on the first floor. He had debated telling Jessica what he was doing, but he didn't need to upset or alarm her. She was worried enough about the baby. "Hi, Nurse Prichard."

"Hello, Dr. Matthews. How are you?"

"Good. I need a couple of radios and the keys to one of the vans." He shifted the backpack on his shoulder. She looked at the checkout sheet in front of her and frowned. "I don't see your name listed as one of the crews going out today."

Thomas smiled. He knew that if she checked the reserves, it would list him and Luke and give them clearance to go out any time. "Check the reserve sheet."

She turned the page, ran her finger down the list, and came across his name. "Is Luke joining you today?"

Luke came running up. "Here I am. Sorry. Had to promise the wife I'd try to make it back in one piece."

Thomas slapped Luke on the back and gave him a knowing smile. He knew Luke had led everyone who was going out to the parking garage. Tara had distracted the guard so Luke could sneak them out. They would be ready to jump in the van as soon as Thomas and Luke came to the garage with the keys.

Nurse Prichard reached for a set of keys and two walkies.

"Can we have one more in case one goes out? It happened last time."

"Sure." She hands them a third walkie.

Thomas and Luke headed down the hall and rounded the corner. Jacob was waiting for them. Luke handed him a walkie. "Keep it on four. We'll radio you as soon as we get a subject."

Jacob nodded, turned his wheelchair around, and headed back down the corridor.

Thomas put his hand on Luke's shoulder. "Let's go. We're wasting daylight. It seems to get dark fast."

The two headed to the garage. They got there and saw Tara still chatting up the guard. Thomas and Luke saluted the guard as they walked past. The guard acknowledged them and returned his attention to Tara. The guys got into the van and drove to where the others were hiding. Luke opened the door, and they jumped, including Lucy and Sammy. "Hey! What's the deal? You two aren't supposed to be here."

The girls look guilty. Thomas looked back. "Too late. We gotta go."

Luke shut the door, and Thomas drove out of the garage to the guard post. Privates Patterson and Watson opened the gate to let them out of the hospital grounds. Private Patterson looked after the van and gave a double take. He could have sworn he had seen a kid at the window.

Lucy quickly ducked down. Luke angrily looked at the girls. "What gives? I told you I'd look for the boy."

Lucy looked away embarrassed. When she turned back, her eyes had gone golden again. "I know, but I got a feeling, and I just needed to come. I'm sorry." Luke opened his mouth to say something else, but he felt a hand on his shoulder. He looked into Jessie's green eyes and simply shut his mouth. He joined Thomas up front.

"We brought everything we need, right? I mean, what we'll need to subdue the subject so we can sneak him or her into the hospital."

"Yep. I have a syringe of Diprivan," Sammy said.

"What's Diprivan?"

"An anesthetic used to put people to sleep before surgery."

"We sure it's going to work on a zombie?"

"We're not sure of anything. That's why we also brought zip ties, and we're going to find a pet store to get a muzzle."

Everyone was quiet as Thomas headed toward High Street. He turned into the alley and immediately ran into zombies. Thomas quickly reversed the van. At least fifteen zombies started following them. Thomas made a U-turn around the corner. The others saw the zombies fade into the distance as the van sped up.

Thomas made two left turns and then another into the same alley but from the other end. The coast seemed clear—no zombies in sight. "Man, that was close."

Luke looked up and down the alley and saw some movement behind a dumpster. "Stop. I think I see something."

Thomas put the van in park. Luke carefully opened the door and got out. He walked to the dumpster and looked behind it. He saw a boy about ten scrunched down against the wall. "Hey, kiddo, it's okay. You can come out. I won't hurt you. The zombies are gone." He beckoned the boy, who timidly rose from his crouch and walked toward Luke. They heard some scratching coming from the dumpster. The boy quickly moved to Luke's side. Pete looked out the window. "Look out! It's a zombie!" Luke snatched up the boy and ran to the van. They made it in just as the horde of zombies came around the corner. The one in the dumpster whose clothes looked like they had seen better days joined the group as they attacked the van. "Move it!"

Thomas backed up out of the alley and made a hard left as soon as he was clear of the alley. They breathed sighs of relief. "They seem to be in sync. As soon as one saw me, the others came around the corner."

Luke looked at the boy in his arms. "Hello. What's your name?"

The boy moved out of Luke's embrace and sat next to Jessie. "Tyler. Thanks for the rescue. I thought I was a goner."

"Not a problem. How long were you trapped behind that dumpster?"

"Since yesterday. I had to hide because my family had all become zombies. They didn't notice me. The one in the dumpster was my sister. We were looking for food when we were attacked. I got away without a scratch, but my mom and sister didn't. They thought they were okay, but as soon as we got back to our hiding place, they couldn't breathe and they started turning pale. In a few minutes, I couldn't recognize them. Right before she changed completely, she yelled at me to run, so I did, and I hid behind the dumpster. I figured they were going to get me."

"I'm Luke. The lovely lady you're sitting next to is my wife, Jessie. The Bobbsey Twins over there are Sammy and Lucy. Thomas is our stunt driver. The guys are Pete, Shawn, and Lyle. Okay, guys, we need to get to a pet store for a muzzle."

Tyler froze after hearing that. Jessie touched his shoulder. "Relax. The muzzle isn't for you. We're experimenting with zombies. We need to know if they're what the books say or if maybe there's a cure. We just don't want to become contaminated."

Tyler still looked a little apprehensive, but he nodded at that explanation.

Thomas turned right on the next street. At the end of the block was a pet store. He pulled up to the front and was prepared to jump out. "Wait. Someone's inside," Luke said.

They all looked and saw someone inside moving slowly and jerkily.

"Looks like a zombie." Thomas grabbed his backpack and took out the hypodermic needle. He gestured to Luke to come with him. "The rest of you stay here. We're going in. Maybe this will be enough to knock it out." Very slowly and quietly, the two of them got out of the van and stayed low as they approached the door. Thomas turned the knob. The bell above the door jingled. The zombie turned around and started to shuffle to the door. Thomas threw the door open. "Move!"

Thomas and Luke charged in and played keep-away with the zombie. "Hurry up! We know they have the ability to alert others."

Luke drew the zombie's attention as Thomas got around in the back of her. Recognition showed on the zombie's and Luke's faces. "Lacy?"

The zombie held her arms out as if she were trying to embrace Luke. Thomas stuck the needle in her neck. She screamed, but then she became dizzy and collapsed into Thomas's arms. The two carried her outside. Jessie threw open the back door, and they loaded her in. Jessie bound her hands with twist ties. "I need to go back for a muzzle."

Sammy looked out the window and saw a horde of zombies headed their way. She noticed that even though they moved slowly, they were not nearly as slow as the books said zombies were. And they seemed to be communicating with each other that something just didn't seem right. "Thomas! They are coming!"

Thomas looked up and saw at least twenty zombies headed their way. He jumped into the driver's seat, backed up, made a U-turn, and sped off in the opposite direction. The horde couldn't keep up.

Lucy let out a nervous laugh. "Man! MacGyver has nothing on you."

Pete, Lyle, and Shawn laughed.

"What? Who?"

"I like to watch old shows. My parents subscribed to the ancient TV show channel, and I kinda got hooked on it."

That made the guys laugh louder.

The zombie started thrashing around. "She's waking up."

"What? I gave her enough to knock out an elephant for hours. There's another syringe in my backpack. Hurry up and give it to her." Jessie grabbed the backpack and rummaged through it for the syringe. She got ready to plunge it into her neck. The zombie's eyes popped open, and she looked straight at Sammy, who was sitting a little too close. The zombie reached out, scratched Sammy, and uttered, "*Luuuuke.*" Jessie shoved the needle into her neck, and she collapsed again. Sammy stared in horror at the scratch on her arm. Jessie rummaged through the backpack again and came out with a bandage that she wrapped around Sammy's arm. Tyler started to whimper and cower in the corner of the van behind the passenger side. He reached for the door handle. "Let me out! She's going to turn!"

Shawn grabbed his hand. "Dude, calm down. We're almost at the hospital."

Tyler started crying violently and pressed his face into Shawn's chest. Thomas turned to Luke. "We need to contact the others. We need a diversion."

Luke got on the walkie. "Jacob."

"Jacob here. What's up, guys?"

"We're almost there. We need a diversion."

"Copy that. The guard who has a crush on Tara is still on duty. She'll distract him."

"I need a gurney. We need to get our subject to the morgue."

Sammy started to wheeze violently.

"We need an oxygen tank too."

"What's going on?"

"No time to answer. Just take care of what I said."

"Copy that. Securing items and creating diversion now."

Thomas slowed down as he approached the gate. Tyler's sobs subsided to hiccups. Everyone hid under the sheets and lay perfectly still. Luke picked up the hysterical child and got into the passenger seat with him. The guards opened the gate just as Luke got situated.

Private Patterson looked out the window and saw the crying boy in Luke's lap. "Bringing in another one I see."

Luke gave the guard a weary smile. "Yeah. He was hiding behind a dumpster. He's a little frightened. We need to get him inside and calm him down."

"Copy that." Patterson motioned to the other guard to let them through.

They drove through the gate and breathed a sigh of relief as the soldiers secured the gates behind them. Thomas drove into the garage, parked, and looked around for Jacob. What he saw was not what he had expected. Jessica was coming toward him with a gurney and an oxygen tank. Luke followed Thomas's gaze. "Oh man. You're in trouble."

Thomas flashed him a dirty look and opened his door. "Hi, honey."

Jessica looked at him with an expression that could have melted the tires on the van. Jessie threw open the doors.

"No time to chat. Sammy needs oxygen."

Jessica gave Jessie the oxygen, who put the mask over Sammy's face and adjusted the flow until she began to breathe normally again.

"Can you walk?"

Sammy nodded enthusiastically, and Jessie helped her out of the van. Everyone else got out. Jessica noticed the unconscious zombie lying on the floor of the van and yelled, "Are you fuckin' crazy?"

"Shhh. I'll explain later. Let's just get her on the gurney. We need to get her into the morgue."

Jessica hissed, "Fine, but I demand a full explanation."

"Fine. Can we go now?"

Thomas, Shawn, Jessica, Lyle, and Pete lifted the unconscious zombie out of the van and onto the gurney as Tara kept on distracting the guard. They wheeled her past the two and into the hospital.

Chapter 14

The morgue was cold, creepy, nightmarish. The gang placed the zombie on a slab. The silence was deafening. Jessica cleared her throat. "I hate to interrupt this pity party, but someone needs to tell me what's going on."

Everyone looked at Thomas for an explanation. "Great. It wasn't my idea, but I gotta explain."

Lucy giggled. "In the immortal words of Ricky Ricardo, 'Lucy, you got some 'splainin' to do.'" Everyone looked at Lucy, and she cracked up. The tension in the room dissipated.

Jessica uncrossed her arms and relaxed. "Okay, I'm listening."

Thomas started to speak, but Luke held up his hand. "It's okay, Thomas. This was my idea. I'll do the talking."

"It's okay. I agreed to it," Thomas said.

The door to the morgue banged open, and Jacob wheeled himself in, followed by Tara. "Hey, guys." Jacob, obviously frazzled, looked at Thomas. "Sorry, man. She demanded an explanation. I didn't have a choice. Besides, I wasn't sure how I was going to get a gurney and portable oxygen tank to you."

"It's cool. She's not easily dissuaded when she's on a mission. We were just about to explain the mission. Join us. Shut the door."

Everyone got comfortable.

"You have to admit these zombies are strange," Thomas said. "We're not dealing with fiction. This is real life, and some crazy shit's going on. I mean, this zombie for instance knew Luke. She responded to him. She even said his name before passing out. The disease is spread by a bite or scratch. Also, if they get oxygen immediately, they don't evolve into zombie-like creatures. Exhibit A, Sammy."

Jessica looked at Sammy as realization began to dawn on her. "Are you saying Sammy got scratched? If she hadn't gotten the oxygen in time she would have become a zombie?"

"Yes, that's exactly what I'm saying."

Jessica suddenly couldn't catch her breath. "That means when Kylie scratched me, she infected our child. I don't understand why she isn't a zombie. Why was her scratch toxic?"

"I'm thinking. Go with me on this. She's still fighting the infection, so she's still contagious. I'm not sure if the oxygen is delaying the inevitable. Maybe the oxygen is making the virus obsolete. I'm still not sure how some of us got infected and some of us didn't. Let's look at the day it all began. The electrical storm. The black rain. When my family and I were watching the news report, we saw a news reporter become a zombie. She'd gotten wet from the rain. We were running inside, and Kylie got wet. Her jacket had a hole in it. After the news reporter turned, Kylie had trouble breathing. She has severe asthma. We have a portable oxygen tank available in case of a very severe allergic reaction. We put her on oxygen, and I adjusted the dose, and she began to breathe normally. A few days later, Thomas and Shawn show up. They bought us here. Kylie then began her fevers and lapsed into a coma."

"That makes sense. Not everyone got hit by the rain. We need blood samples so we can see what's affecting them. I'll need a needle, blood vial, tourniquet, and alcohol swabs."

They rummaged around in the morgue and collected the items. Jessica applied the tourniquet. Amazingly, a vein popped up. She swabbed it with alcohol and drew two vials of dark-red and thick blood. She released the tourniquet and applied a bandage. The zombie began to stir. They all held their breath. The zombie settled down and seemed to be sleeping.

"That was strange. We need to make sure the zombie—"

"Lacy."

"What?"

"Her name's Lacy."

"Okay, we need to make sure Lacy's hooked up to an

IV drip that will keep her sedated. We don't want to be the reason everyone in the hospital gets infected. We also need to get Sammy a room so she's comfortable. If she's anything like Kylie, she'll soon run a fever and possibly lapse into a coma."

"I'll take Sammy. I need to check on our child. I'll get the IV drip and a microscope so we can look at her blood closely."

Jessica, Sammy, and Lucy head out the door. The silence in the room made everyone uncomfortable. Luke looked at Jessie; she seemed hurt at Luke's admitting to knowing the zombie. He walked over to her and whispered something to her. She gave him an angry and hurt look before heading for the door. He silently followed.

"What was that all about?" Jacob asked.

"Not sure, man, but something tells me it's not good."

Luke followed Jessie down the hall. She finally stopped and put her head in her hands. Her brown, shoulder-length hair fell over her hands as her body began to shake. Luke came up behind her and engulfed her in his arms. She turned, put her arms around him, and buried her head in his neck. He kissed her head and breathed in her scent—almond cookies.

Jessie gave him a weak smile. "I know it looks like I'm upset with you. I'm not. I just didn't think I would come face-to-face with the woman you had an affair with. I'm just shedding the hurt I guess I still feel. I promised you I'd move on from this, and I will."

He took her chin in his hands and tilted her head up to kiss her.

Jessica came around the corner with a microscope, slides, and a dropper. Lucy was following her with an IV. She passed Jessie and Luke giving them a quizzical look. They follow her back into the morgue.

Thomas and Jessica were setting up a portable lab. Jessica withdrew some blood from a vial with a dropper and squeezed some onto a slide. She placed another slide on top of it smearing the blood sample. She slipped the slides under the microscope and adjusted the focus. "Now that's strange. Look. Tell me what you see."

Thomas peered into the microscope. "I see very healthy red blood cells being attacked by dark-red cells that look almost black. And misshapen. Too bad we don't have a different blood sample to compare it with."

Jessica reached into the pocket of her lab coat and produced a vial of blood. "I took the liberty of drawing some of Kylie's blood."

She set up a pair of slides with a drop of Kylie's blood on a slide and placed it under the microscope. "That is definitely interesting. Just like Lacy, Kylie seems to have two different types of red blood cells fighting each other. The difference is Kylie's second blood cells are a bright red I'm guessing from the extra oxygen she's receiving. There seems to be a lot more of them, and they're multiplying. By the looks of things, Kylie's blood cells are almost completely taking over."

"What does that mean? Is my sister going to mutate?

Is she going to become one of those things?" Jessie pointed a shaking finger at Lacy.

Jessica looked at Jessie. "I don't think so. If my theory is correct, Lacy's condition is due to the lack of oxygen, but Kylie's situation is different. I don't know what's going to happen once the blood cells take over. This is a wait-and-see game."

Jessie's hand gravitated toward her mouth to stifle a scream. "Oh God!"

"Relax. We can't panic here. Thomas and I are in the same boat. Our child is infected as well." Jessica suddenly placed a hand on her chest.

"Are you all right?"

"I suddenly have trouble catching my breath."

Lyle brought over a chair. "Sit down for a minute. You had a baby yesterday."

Jessica began to wheeze. "Quick—down the hall to your left is where we keep oxygen tanks. The code is two three six seven. Hurry!"

Pete raced out the door and quickly returned with an oxygen tank. Thomas put the mask over Jessica's face and turned the oxygen up about 10 percent; she started breathing normally. Everyone was so concerned with Jessica that they didn't notice Lacy stir.

"The scratch must now be affecting Jessica. It took its time, but I'm guessing that was because of the pregnancy, and the baby was infected first. It took a little more time getting into her bloodstream."

A loud clunking noise prompted everyone to look

at Lacy, who had gotten off the slab and was heading toward Luke.

"Dammit! We forgot to hook her up to the IV! Move! Try to navigate to the door."

A lot of medical equipment was in the way. Lacy knocked over the microscope; the slides fell out and broke on the floor. The door was opened, and everyone backed out. Jessica had a little trouble because of the oxygen tank, but Thomas managed to slam the door shut just as Lacy got to it, essentially trapping her inside.

Lacy was fumbling with the doorknob as a soldier came around the corner. He looked in the window of the morgue and reached for his gun.

"No! Don't shoot her! Do you have a tranquilizer gun? We need to subdue her."

The soldier was dumbfounded, but he grabbed his walkie and radioed for help.

Lacy wandered away from the door and tried to pick up objects around her. She seemed to become even more agitated because she didn't know how to use her hands. She came back to the door and started pounding on the glass.

Several soldiers came around the corner. The sergeant told them to fire through the glass. Everyone screamed as the bullets flew. One went through the glass and hit Lacy squarely in the forehead. Blood splattered on the wall. Lacy fell to the floor.

"Open the door! Let's get this zombie out of here."

Someone was crying. The sergeant turned to the

group. "What just happened here? I need everyone upstairs and in my office *now*!"

Shawn helped Tara up. Pete picked up Lucy, who was crying so hard that she couldn't walk on her own. The rest of them follow the sergeant out of the basement.

Chapter 15

Sergeant Johanson opened the door to what obviously had been a doctor's office—credentials were hanging on the wall and medical journals were piled on the floor. She gestured to the chairs and couch and looked at them for an explanation. Everyone began to talk at once. The sergeant whistled and said, "One at a time!"

Luke said, "I know we made a dangerous call by bringing her here, but we needed to know for sure if these zombies were like those in fiction."

The sergeant crossed her arms. "I see. And pray tell what did you find out?"

"They're alive, for one," Thomas said. "And they have a primitive understanding of their surroundings. We think this is because of the lack of oxygen they received during the metabolic change they went through."

"Am I to believe those creatures are human beings who are alive and need help?" the sergeant asked.

"Yes!" Lucy just about screamed.

Luke put his arms around her "It's okay, Lucy. Calm down. We can get our point across without yelling."

She hung her head in defeat and suddenly looked very tired. "Sorry. This is just so frustrating."

Sergeant Johanson paced the room arms behind her back. "What else do I need to know?" Not wanting to draw conclusions for the sergeant, no one answered her at first. Raising her eyebrows, the sergeant looked at everyone. They all squirmed.

Except for Lyle. "Were you listening when Thomas said lack of oxygen? Do I need to spell this out for you? You're a sergeant in the army! You can't make the easiest connection?" He threw up his hands. "Kylie, the baby Trisha, and now Sammy and Jessica all require heavy doses of oxygen."

Realization began to dawn on the sergeant. "Are you telling me these people are infected with whatever has turned people into zombies?"

"Bingo. By George, I think she's got it," Lyle replied.

She gave Lyle a stern look. "Where are Sammy and the baby?"

"Sammy's in the same room as Kylie, and Trisha is still in the NICU," Thomas said.

Sergeant Johanson walked to the door. "Escort Dr. Jessica Matthews to room 201, and make sure her baby is placed in the same room. I want an around-the-clock protection detail placed in that room. No one is allowed in without my permission. Are we clear?"

"Yes Sergeant," the soldiers said. They escorted the doctor out of the room and down the hall.

Thomas shouted, "What are you doing? They're not a threat."

"I can't take that chance," the sergeant said. "I won't put the people here in unnecessary danger. You're lucky I'm not having you all court martialed for this."

"We're not in the army. This is *not* a police state. We're fighting to survive in a world that's been invaded by zombies. We need to find a cure, not cause panic, which is what you're doing by having a guard posted outside the door of a room full of sick people."

"Doctor, I'm in charge here. The world is in chaos, and it's my job to make sure everyone who isn't infected or a zombie is safe. You can continue to experiment and maybe find a cure for this zombie virus, which according to you has infected the creatures out there and apparently a few in here."

"Don't call them creatures. They're human beings who have been turned into zombie-like creatures. They have just as much right to breathe as we do."

"We'll see about that. What do you need from me?"

"Another infected person since you just had the last one shot in the head."

"I'll send out soldiers to get you another zombie. How did you secure the last one?"

"We dosed her with Diprivan, kind of like morphine. It knocks them out. They require a very high dosage. Two needles full of the stuff should work. Then we need to make sure they're hooked up to an IV of the same stuff to keep them under. That's where we messed up."

"Fine. Get the supplies ready."

She opened the door, and everyone shuffled out. Thomas said, "I want access to the room where my wife and the others are."

"Fine, Doctor. You can examine them. I think it's best if you're the only doctor tending to them right now."

"I want to visit my sister."

"I'm not sure that's a good idea at the moment."

"Why? She isn't a threat to me. She's in a coma for goodness' sake. She's my sister!"

The sergeant threw up her hands in defeat. "Fine, but you assume the risk. I won't be held responsible for anything that might happen and especially if you get contaminated."

"Fine."

The group walked down the hall and entered the waiting room on the first floor. Thomas closed the door. They all sat. "So we can now do this experiment without hiding it. I'm going to need help now that Jessica's incapacitated. Are you guys up for the challenge?"

Everyone nodded. Jacob asked, "What can I do? I'm wheelchair bound."

Thomas examined Jacob's ankle. "Looks like I can put a walking cast on this. I'll x-ray it to be sure."

Jacob's face lit up like a Christmas tree. "Really?"

"Yeah," Thomas said as he pushed Jacob's wheelchair

toward the door, which Pete opened. "Stay here. We'll be right back."

As Thomas and Jacob headed out the door, alarms began to ring throughout the hospital. Everyone rushed out into the hall. "What is it?"

Thomas didn't have time to answer. He raced down the hall and up the stairs to the second floor. Everyone quickly followed. "Hey! No fair! I can't take the stairs!" Jacob said as he wheeled over to the elevator.

Thomas reached the room where his family was just in time to see the doctors trying to resurrect Kylie. "Charge to four hundred."

Jessie got to the door just as the doctor said, "Time of death, June 25, 2025, at 5:35 p.m."

A scream could be heard from the doorway. Luke grabbed Jessie as she fought to get to her sister. Everyone was concerned about Jessie; she became incoherent and unable to stand from the shock of her sister's death.

They didn't notice Kylie sitting up in her bed. "What's going on? Why's my sister upset?"

The guards quickly drew their guns and pointed them at Kylie. "Whoa! Why the hell are you pointing those things at me?"

Shaking, a nurse walked over to the dresser and picked up a hand mirror to give to Kylie. She stepped back as if she had just been bitten. Kylie smirked and held up the mirror. Someone screamed. It took Kylie a bit to realize she was the one doing the screaming. Her left eye was its usual blue, but her right eye was red. She gulped.

"Out of my way!" Sergeant Johanson pushed her way through the crowd to Kylie's bedside. "What's going on?"

Dr. Crane said, "Kylie experienced a very high fever that sent her into convulsions that stopped her heart. We tried to get her heart started again. Unfortunately, we weren't able to. I called time of death."

"Really, Doctor? She seems pretty alive to me."

"When we were consoling her sister, she sat up and started talking as if she hadn't died."

"I see. And the red eye?"

"I think a full exam is necessary at this time," Thomas said.

"I agree, Doctor. Keep me apprised."

The sergeant left. They heard the piercing cries of a hungry infant.

Chapter 16

A knock at the door. "Come in."

In walked a female soldier. "Sergeant, there's a Dr. Foster on the walkie. I'm not sure how he got the frequency, but he insists on talking to whoever's in charge."

The sergeant took the walkie. "This is Sergeant Johanson. Dr. Foster is it?"

"Yes, Sergeant. It's good to know we're not alone out here. I have some interesting news about the atmosphere. Can we meet?"

"Where are you?"

"At the Omega Observatory on Mt. Sumi overlooking Greenburger Bay."

"I know where that is. It's just a few clicks south of the military base. There are zombies everywhere. I'm not sure how we can get to you, Doctor." Silence. "Dr. Foster, are you there?"

"Yes, Sergeant. I was just thinking about the zombies

outside. We had to board up the glass doors so they won't know we're here."

"Did you say *we*, Doctor? How many people are with you?"

"Fifteen. We're running out of food. I'm afraid that if we start to starve and die off, the threat will be inside, not outside."

"We're fully stocked here and could easily accommodate your group. I'll gather some soldiers and a few volunteers. They can be there in about two hours. I need your group to be ready to make a run for it. If you need to bring anything, make it small."

"Understood. We'll be ready."

The sergeant hit her intercom button. "Private Lebsion, gather the troops and almost all the search groups in the cafeteria."

"You said almost all the search groups?"

"Yes. Leave out the team that includes Dr. Matthews and Luke Epson. They have pressing matters here."

"Understood, Sergeant. Will take care of this immediately. What should I tell them?"

"Just that there's an emergency meeting. That'll be all, Private."

Dr. Foster placed his walkie in the charging cradle and turned to the people standing anxiously waiting for the word. "Gather only small items. Be ready to hightail it out of here. The sergeant has agreed to send us help. They have food and shelter. They'll be here in two hours to pick us up. Dr. Sote, Dr. Carver, and Dana, please gather the information we have stored on flash drives and laptops. Everyone else, gather your things. Be back here in an hour. It's time to get out of this place."

Everyone dispersed as quickly as they had assembled to gather equipment and necessities. Dr. Foster took a deep breath and felt some relief at the prospect of getting to a safer area with food and shelter. The zombies would no longer be an immediate threat.

He headed out the door. He thought that if he was reading the barometer correctly, an impending change in the atmosphere was about to wreak havoc on Earth. He felt that did not bode well for any organism.

Two hours later, he heard pounding on the boarded-up glass door. The doctor looked out the small peephole and saw a few dozen people with guns. He and others pried the boards off the door.

"Dr. Foster I presume," someone said, and the doctor nodded. "It's clear right now, but I don't know for how long. Everyone into the vans as quickly as possible. We need to move."

The group raced to the vans and piled inside. Zombies began emerging from the trees and bushes around the observatory. The drivers headed for the mountain road. As they pulled away, Dr. Foster took a last look at the observatory and felt sadness, relief, and regret. The others in his van gave off shouts of relief.

Privates Patterson and Carrigan unlocked the hospital gates for the convoy of vans. When the last van entered, they heard a strange sound. A zombie who had ridden on the roof of the last van jumped down and charged Private Carrigan. The private was battling him when Private Patterson put a bullet in the zombie's head but not before Private Carrigan was bitten by a zombie.

Other soldiers ran to his aid. He backed up, looking at the blood dripping from his arm, and started having trouble breathing. He put his pistol to his head, pulled the trigger, and fell to the ground. The others quickly secured the gates and carried the fallen soldier through the hospital doors. No one noticed a few zombies looking on with bewildered looks on their faces. Strange as it may seem, they looked as though they understood what had just happened. They shuffled away.

A screeching sound coming from the hospital caused the new arrivals to cower. "What was that?" one asked.

Someone down the hallway yelled, "That came from special residents on the second floor. No need for alarm. They scream whenever there are zombies around."

Sergeant Johanson and Nurse Prichard came around the corner and faced the new people. "Hello. I'm Sergeant Johanson."

Dr. Foster shook her hand and introduced himself and the others.

"I'm sure everyone is hungry and tired," the sergeant said. "Let's get everyone settled. The cafeteria is to the left down this hall. Shower stalls are to the right of the cafeteria, and just a few doors down is what we call the store, where you'll find clothing, towels, soap, and shampoo. Help yourselves. When you've eaten and showered, we'll get you rooms. Just check with Nurse Prichard here."

"Sergeant, I'm curious about your special patient."

"Very well, Doctor. I was hoping you were. If you and the other scientists would follow me please."

Dr. Foster, Dr. Soto, Dr. Carver, and Dana followed the sergeant to the elevator and up to the second floor.

Chapter 17

The sergeant and the others entered room 201. Thomas was giving Kylie a full checkup. She turned to face the door.

"Oh crap! What the hell's wrong with her eye?" Dana asked.

Kylie laughed. "That was rude. Do you usually just blurt things out before you think?"

Dana bit her lip. "Sorry, but your eye caught me off guard. I didn't mean to offend you."

"It's all right. I'm not used to it either."

"Please forgive my daughter," Dr. Foster said. "Even as a child, she always blurted out whatever she felt."

"Was that you who screamed?"

"No. This time it was Sammy."

The curtain separating the beds was pulled aside so everyone could see Sammy, who was hooked up to an oxygen tank.

"Is she all right?"

Thomas looked up from checking Kylie's heartbeat

or in this case two heartbeats. "Yes, she's fine. She's going through the second phase of the metamorphosis."

"Metamorphosis?"

"Yes. It seems that within a week, anyone who gets scratched and was given oxygen fairly quickly goes through this. They lapse into a coma for a month. Then they die so to speak and come back with some physical changes you see and some you don't. My wife, our child, and Sammy have all entered what I'm calling the sleep phase. They'll have high fevers, but we'll give them more oxygen. Kylie here has gone through the change. The results are larger lung capacity, two hearts, and a red eye."

The doctors pondered that.

"That would explain the change in the atmosphere. The oxygen level has flattened out at 50 percent, but that's way above normal. That would also explain the physical change in Kylie. In order for her to breathe, her body needs to adapt. Without this adaptation, humans would slowly become extinct. The more oxygen we breathe, the harder it is on our lungs and hearts. These organs would have to pump twice as hard to allow for the intake of oxygen. Eventually, anyone not like these four here will find it harder to breathe. Sure, we can do things faster, but we will exhaust ourselves quicker.

"Kylie used to be asthmatic, but since this change, she doesn't need any oxygen or her inhaler. I had her on the treadmill thirty minutes ago. I've never seen anyone run that fast for that long and not be out of breath. Her heartbeat was normal as well. She was running fifty miles a minute. A *minute*—not an hour. It was incredible."

Kylie was the first to break the silence that remark had caused. "So we need to find a cure for the zombies still roaming around. We also need to find an easier, or at least quicker, way for everyone to morph into me."

"That seems to be right. Wait. Did you say 'cure' for the zombies? How do you cure something that's dead?"

Kylie and Thomas laughed, but the sergeant wasn't amused. Dana gave them a dirty look. "What's so funny? He asked a legitimate question."

"Sorry. I guess you wouldn't know. The zombies aren't dead. They're living, breathing humans who didn't receive the extra oxygen to slow the process down. They became what you see. We're not sure yet why they became these zombie-like creatures. What we do know is that they have two types of red blood cells. The abnormal ones are overtaking the normal ones. The lack of extra oxygen might account for the second set of red blood cells being dark red, almost black. The blood cells had to adapt quickly, and it caused the wrong metamorphosis to happen."

"You know this to be true?"

Thomas put his stethoscope around his neck and walked to the door. "I have all the answers to your questions in the lab down the hall. Follow me. I'll make sure you see firsthand what we've been talking about."

Kylie pulled back her sheet and got out of her bed.

"Should she be doing that?"

"She's fine. This half of the hospital is closed off to anyone not authorized. Kylie has been helping with the experiment ever since she changed. Follow me."

They headed to the lab and entered. Dana jumped and tried not to scream. The others follow her gaze to a gurney on which what appeared to be a zombie was hooked up to an IV.

"What in the world is that?"

"A zombie who's medicated and being kept strapped down. Come, doctors. I have four microscopes set up. One has blood drawn from Kylie in her new state, one has blood from the zombie, one has blood from Sammy, and the last one has my blood. You can see each stage and how each one differs."

The doctors looked through the microscopes. The first one showed Kylie's bright-red blood cells, which looked extremely healthy. The second one showed the zombie's dark-red and misshapen cells that were turning blacker by the second. The third showed regular blood cells being taken and changed by the bright-red blood cells. The fourth one showed normal human blood cells—no mutations.

"You can see, Doctors, that different mutations are happening. We're hoping to take these zombie blood cells and hopefully send them on the right path."

"Why not just introduce oxygen to the mix?"

"Tried that. My theory is that they've already mutated and that introducing oxygen into their bloodstream would make no difference."

"How about giving them some of Kylie's blood?"

"Tried that too. They react violently and become ill in seconds. They die quickly, and once dead, they stay that way. We think Kylie's blood is the cure, but we have to dilute it or mix it for it to work. We've been at this for only a week."

Dr. Foster rolled up his sleeves. "Time to get to work. Let's find a cure and save the world."

Chapter 18

The door opened. Jessica walked in and saw frustration on Dr. Foster's face. "Is there a problem, Doctor?"

He sighed heavily. "I can't seem to get the combination right. I've tried more of Kylie's blood and mixed a different amount with the infected blood cells from the zombies. The results are the same. It destroys all the blood cells. I don't want to keep destroying these living dead. They expire quickly."

"It's been only three months, Jonathan. Be patient. You'll figure it out. Take a break. Get something to eat. Refueling is necessary."

Jonathan looked into Jessica's eyes. One was its normal brown, but the other was red, the result of the change. That took some getting used to on his part. Jessica smiled. They headed out the door.

Thomas was coming down the hall holding Trisha. She giggled as her father skipped down the hall. Jessica asked, "How are my favorite people doing today?"

Trisha reached for her mom. "I'm good. Daddy too."

One of the most amazing things to happen with the metamorphosis was that Trisha was able to speak almost immediately. She was in the rudimentary stages of forming sentences, but she seemed to be able to understand and answer simple questions.

Kylie and Sammy had both learned three languages during the three months; learning seemed to have become much easier for them. Jessica quickly became knowledgeable in other areas of medicine to the point that she could perform surgery on adults and infants alike, and she was studying the human brain.

"That's wonderful. Now you know you can walk."

"I know."

Jessica put her daughter on the floor. It seemed strange at first, but Trisha went through many stages in months. When she woke up from her coma, she could sit up and roll over. By month two, she could crawl. By month three, she was walking, but only on the second floor; the sergeant wasn't allowing her to go anywhere else.

The sergeant watched the interaction from a monitor in her office. She thought a four-month-old shouldn't be able to do the things Trisha was doing, and she refused to believe either of the transformations was natural. She would have preferred to rid the world of both abominations. She packed her office. She hoped one day the world would return to normal. She looked out the window and saw that the sky was bluer and the sun was brighter. In the past three months, she has noticed other changes in the outside world. Plants had grown taller, and a few of the animals they had come across had morphed into what Kylie and the others had.

The doctors said that the animals were able to adapt to the environment because they had the natural ability to do so while humans did not adapt as well; they needed an extra push in the right direction.

The sergeant shook her head in disbelief. She had kept the existence of the mega humans hidden from most of the survivors. Only the few who were there from the beginning knew. *This cannot be how humans were supposed to live,* she thought. If it was the last thing she did, she would make the world the way she knew it should be. There was no way she was going to adapt or in her opinion lie down and die. Humans were at the top of the food chain. Ceasing to exist was not an option. She pounded her desk. "No!"

Her intercom buzzed. "Are you all right, Sergeant?"

"I'm fine, Private. Please mind your own business."

"I apologize, Sergeant."

She put her head in her hands. She knew she had to stop this evolution from occurring. First, she had to rid the hospital of the four upstairs, even the child, whom the sergeant didn't consider a child, just another being that needed to be eradicated.

She started forming a plan. She needed to be patient. She needed a few recruits who believed as she did. It might take a while, but she was determined to reclaim this place for humans from the four strange beings upstairs and the flesh-eating ones outside.

She hit the intercom button. "Private Malick?"

"Yes Sergeant?"

"Send me Privates Patterson, Sanchez, and McLain, and Corporals Jenkins and Lemmons."

"Yes Sergeant, right away."

The sergeant stood, straightened her uniform, and breathed deeply. In her mind, what she was about to do would save the human race. She didn't realize that for the human race to survive, humans needed to adapt.

A knock on the door. "Come in." In walked the soldiers she had sent for. They saluted her, and she gestured for them to sit. "I've called you here today to discuss an urgent matter. The human race is on the very brink of extinction. You're good soldiers who I know believe as I do. We are standing between the human race and those things in this hospital and outside. We need to devise a plan to rid the world of both abominations."

The soldiers nodded. One of them, however, did not believe as the others did, but he knew he needed to keep a cool head and play along. He was sure the sergeant had gone off the deep end. He considered her a career soldier who could not wrap her brain around changes in the world. Private Patterson knew adaptation was necessary. The fate of the dinosaurs had taught him that. He was determined to find a way to stop her from becoming the end of humanity, which needed to find a way to move forward. Until then, he decided to just keep his head down and calmly follow orders.

"We'll meet again after I've devised a plan. Until then, I don't want this discussed in front of civilians."

She dismissed them. As Private Patterson was walking out, he glimpsed her sinister look and devious smile.

Chapter 19

"This lady is fuckin' crazy." Bryce grabbed his walkie as he and his partner hid behind the car. Glass shattered as a blast from a shotgun went off.

"Get the hell of my property!"

Bryce popped his head up to look through the back windshield of the car. "Look, lady. We're here to help you. We can take you someplace safe."

Chynna Clark looked at Bryce. She had a crazy, mad look in her eyes. "I'm safe. I don't need to be going anywhere with the likes of you. I'm going to give you the count of three to get the hell off my property before I put some buckshot in your ass! One ... two ..." She raised her shotgun.

Bryce and Paul jumped into their car and sped off. Chynna nodded in defiance and set her shotgun by her front door. She walked into the house.

"Well hello, pretty lady."

Chynna spun around and saw three punk rockers in her kitchen; they had multicolored and spiked hair.

One of them was leaning against the sink picking at his fingernails with a pocket knife. Chynna backed up until she felt the barrel of her shotgun sticking into her back; a fourth intruder had snuck in the front and had grabbed her shotgun.

He said, "We're at a crossroads here. The way I see it, you can be a gracious host and show us a good time, or we can force you to be a gracious host. Either way, we'll have a good time."

Chynna wasn't crazy for no reason. Since this whole thing started, she had made sure she could handle every weapon imaginable and knew how to disarm an intruder in a split second. She wasn't a Marines reservist for nothing. She calmly smiled at the men and relaxed; she'd play along. When the one who was holding the shotgun to her back relaxed, she pulled the blade she had in her apron, spun around, and buried it in his chest. She snatched the shotgun out of his hands and blasted the other three before they even moved.

She put the shotgun on the counter and surveyed her handiwork. "I was wondering what I'd have for dinner."

She was only five-four, but she could carry a man twice her size. She took each of the bodies outside and laid them next to a long table that held carving knives, bone saws, and other tools. She stripped them of their clothing and hosed the blood off them. One by one, she dismantled the bodies and put the parts in a gray wash tin beside the bench. When she was done, she washed her hands and fired up her grill. As soon as she had a good amount cooked, she loaded it on a plate and took it to a storage shed in the far corner of her backyard. She pulled a key out of her apron and unlocked the padlock on the door. She heard growling and snarling inside.

She opened the door and switched on the light. Three people were chained to the wall. One was a man about thirty and wearing overalls covered in blood. The other two were children. One was a girl about ten with hair in pigtails; she was wearing a pink dress and a white sweater also covered in blood. The third was a boy about three in blue shorts and a white T-shirt.

"Hello, my sweeties. Dinner!"

She put the food down in front of them. Not one of them reached for her or the plate. The three were Chynna's family. They had been attacked on their way home from the fair. They had made it home just before the change.

Chynna had done what she had to do. She was convinced they were sick. She thought she would have her family back as soon as there was a cure. Until then, she would protect and feed them. As most people did, Chynna believed the fiction about zombies and figured they needed meat but certainly not raw meat; that just wasn't healthy, she felt.

At first, Chynna fed them the animals on her farm. When that supply ran out, she fed them animals from a neighbor's farm. One day, she came across a homeless person who wasn't looking very well. There were no more animals, and she was desperate. *Nobody will miss him*, she had told herself.

She had taken him home and cleaned and fed him before she strangled him. She cried hard at that but told herself it was all for her family. Ever since then, she had been looking for people nobody would miss.

That day was the first day she had experienced any trouble with her victims, but she didn't consider it to have been that much trouble.

Chynna moved out of their reach, and her family quickly grabbed and consumed the food. She smiled through her tears. "Just a little while longer, dears." She stepped out, turned off the light, and padlocked the shed. She froze the other remains. She pulled out a frozen dinner and put it in the microwave for herself. She felt content. *Just a little while longer and life will return to normal.*

Chapter 20

Tyler looked on from the corner of the waiting room as several children played in the hall. He sat there trying not to cry. He wished he didn't feel like an outcast. He didn't know how to socialize; he felt awkward and shy around others.

He took a deep breath, stood, and headed out to the hall. He opened the exit door leading to the stairs and went to the second floor. When he got to the door, he saw the sign—Do Not Enter. Trespassers Will Be Shot On Sight. Tyler cringed. He put his ear to the door to see if he could hear anything. He pushed the door open and peeked out. He didn't see anyone. He stepped out into the hall and walked toward the source of the laughter he heard.

He opened a room door and was taken aback by what he saw. Trisha was playing with blocks and had built a huge tower. She was standing on a chair trying to reach the top. The chair began to wobble. He rushed into the room just in time to catch her as her tower of blocks collapsed and the chair toppled over. Trisha started wailing.

Thomas rushed in. "What happened?"

Tyler said, "She was standing on a chair trying to add a block to her tower. It started to wobble, so I came in and caught her."

Thomas took Trisha from Tyler's arms and hugged her. Her crying subsided. "What are you doing here, Tyler? How did you get on this floor?"

"I walked through the stairwell door."

"There should have been a guard. Didn't you read the sign?"

"Yes, but no guard was around."

"Well, now that you know, you won't be permitted to leave this floor. Everyone who knows has been quarantined on this floor."

"It's okay. I wasn't having a great time anywhere else. At least I know you guys."

"Daddy, down please."

Tyler was in shock hearing a baby talking.

"Don't be afraid, Tyler. Trisha is small, but she can communicate. She's been enhanced. You know how zombies were once humans. If humans receive oxygen around the time they become infected, they evolve into Trisha. She represents the evolution of humankind."

He set Trisha down. She walked to Tyler, who recoiled for a second but then relaxed.

"Hi, Tyler. Wanna play?"

"Sure. What would you like to play?"

"Blocks."

Tyler laughed and helped Trisha start stacking up her blocks.

"I'll leave you two while I decide how to tell the sergeant we have a new person on this floor," Thomas said.

"What other things can you do?"

"Stuff. I can walk, talk, and play. I'm a kid."

"Are you strong?"

"Mommy says so."

"Cool. I wish I was like you."

Without warning, Trisha bit Tyler.

"Ow! Why'd you do that?"

"You wanted to be like me. I thought I could help you."

Tyler rubbed his arm. "It's okay, but I don't …"

Tyler began to have trouble breathing. Trisha hit a buzzer on her arm to alert her parents that she needed something.

Thomas and Jessica raced in the room. "What's going on?" They saw Tyler having a hard time breathing. "What happened?"

"I bit him. He wanted to be like me."

Jessica stuck her head out the door and yelled, "I need oxygen stat!"

Luke came in with an oxygen tank. Jessica quickly placed the mask on Tyler's face and adjusted the intake. Tyler began to breathe easier.

"Let's get him to a room."

Thomas lifted him up and carried him to the room next door.

"Mommy?"

"Yes sweetheart?"

"I bad?"

"No, honey, you just didn't understand."

Jessica hugged and soothed Trisha. Thomas came back in. He appeared to have aged a few years in just a few minutes.

Lucy walked through the door. "I had a feeling you needed me. Do you?"

Jessica nodded. "Can you watch Trisha for a little bit?"

"Sure, not a problem."

"Be good, Trisha."

"Okay, no bite."

Jessica and Thomas headed to Tyler's room and heard excited and frightened voices inside. Luke asked them, "What the hell just happened?"

"Looks like Trisha's bite infected Tyler."

"How? I thought you said we were no longer infectious after going through the full transformation."

Thomas looked at Kylie. "I can't explain it."

"Maybe just like our blood is deadly to the zombies, our bites can still infect normal humans."

"That would explain why Trisha was able to infect Tyler."

Shawn drew in a deep breath. "This is bad, man. It means that four, now five of us have to be very careful how we interact with normals."

Sammy looked at Shawn. "Normals? Who are you to say who's normal? Maybe we're the new normals and you're obsolete."

"Come on, Sammy. I didn't mean it like that. I was just thinking out loud. Sorry."

Tara walked in. "Hi, guys. Sorry to interrupt, but I just wanted to tell everyone they just dropped off lunch. Oh, and Betsy wants to know if she can play with Trisha."

Jessica shrugged. "Sure, why not."

Shawn looked apprehensive. "I don't know if that's such a good idea after what happened to Tyler."

"It won't happen again. She just wanted to make her new friend happy. She saw what happened. It scared her."

"I'd feel better if there was some supervision in the room."

"Lucy's with them. It'll be okay."

Tara has been listening to the exchange. "Wait. What happened to Tyler?"

"Trisha bit him, and he became infected."

"Her bite's infectious? Uh, yeah—I think I'll eat lunch with the kids and stick around while they play." Tara quickly left.

Right after Pete asked, "So who's going to tell Sergeant Johanson?" the sergeant walked in.

"Tell the sergeant what?" Everyone gulped. "Hello! Tell me what?"

Jessica answered. "Someone found his way to this floor. He started to play with Trisha. She bit him, and he became infected. He's on oxygen right now."

"What?" Everyone cringed. She poked her head out the door and called for the private guarding the door. Private McKay walked in. "Explain how someone got past a guarded door, Private."

Private McKay turned green. "I wasn't aware of anyone getting on the second floor."

"That's obvious. Did you leave your post unguarded at any time?"

The private gulped. "I may have left it for a few minutes to hit the head."

The sergeant gave him a deadly look. "Back to your post, Private. I'll deal with you later."

The private moved faster than the road runner back to his post.

"So Trisha is infectious?" she asked.

"Yeah. It seems that just as we're deadly to the zombies, we can infect humans and turn them into zombies or one of us."

"Great. Just great. This makes matters worse. Not only are you dangerous to zombies, but now you're dangerous to human beings too!"

"Excuse me, Sergeant, but we're human beings."

"In my book, you're anomalies that shouldn't exist. If I had a say in this, you wouldn't. Not only do you have extra organs, but that baby can walk and talk and she's only five months old. I'm sorry, Doctor, but in my opinion, you're not human."

Jessica started to approach the sergeant. The sergeant backed up toward the wall as if frightened. "Now hold on, missy. You do not get to come in here and insult us and talk about my child that way. If anything and I mean *anything* happens to us or my child, you'll be sorry. Do I make myself clear?"

The sergeant reached for the door handle, opened the door, and backed out. "Crystal clear!" The sergeant walked briskly toward the stairs and left the second floor. Everyone clapped and laughed.

"Never come between a momma bear and her cub. Let's go eat."

Chapter 21

T he sergeant paced her office resisting the urge to smash things. The situation was worse than she had thought. Not only were they stronger and faster; they could also infect human beings. She knew she needed to be careful. The threat she had just received had not been idle. The sergeant knew that in her enhanced state, Dr. Jessica Matthews was a threat like no other. She needed to be careful when proceeding. She was still going to go through with her plan. It would take just a little more cunning and planning than she had thought. *Damn it to hell!* the sergeant thought. She had blown her top and had forgotten all her training when she was told the news. She should have known better than to voice her beliefs out loud.

She had always been a hothead. That was what made a great soldier, but that was what got her in hot water a lot with her commanding officer. She had gone through basic twice because she had failed to keep her mouth shut. That was actually a good thing. She learned more, including how to bite her tongue. However, others would have thought she had had no training at all with the way she had blown it a few minutes earlier.

"Calm down, Rachel." That's what her momma always said when she would get mad at her brothers and sisters if they didn't listen to her. She was the oldest of eight and had been expected to care for and discipline the younger ones. It was hard. She had always liked having things neat and orderly, and her siblings were too noisy and messy.

Her mother had had a different view. She always said, "Home is for free expression, not for good impression." That had driven her daddy nuts. He was a commander in the U.S. Coast Guard. Having things nice and tidy was a must. "Good soldiers have to be ready at a moment's notice. They were always presentable and neat and tidy," he told her. She never understood how her father and mother worked together, but they did though. Her momma always made sure her daddy's study was neat, and he respected that she needed chaos in other parts of the house. Opposites attract.

Rachel shrugged at the memories and continued contemplating the situation at hand. The rumbling in her stomach indicated it was chow time. *Nourishing the body nourishes the mind*, she told herself, and she wanted a clear mind. She went to the cafeteria, filled her tray, and went to a small table in the corner from where she could see the whole place. That was how she liked it as the head honcho. It was her show. She squared her shoulders and began to eat. She was unaware of the conversation happening just a few tables over.

Bryce looked up from his tray and asked in general, "Does anyone find it strange that people have disappeared? Also, there's a no trespassing sign on the second floor. I noticed it yesterday."

Paul stopped eating "There's a no trespassing sign on the second floor? Is that all it says?"

"No. It also says trespassers will be shot on sight."

"That's bullshit. Why can't we go to the second floor? Where are all the missing people?"

Everyone at the table nodded in agreement to that. Something wasn't right, and they needed to know.

"I think Paul and I should confront the sergeant and demand some answers." Everyone agreed with that assessment. "It's settled. We'll see the sergeant tomorrow morning. After a good night's sleep, I'll be ready to demand some answers. What do you say, Paul?"

"Agreed."

Marisa was quiet, but she didn't agree with her husband and Paul. True, people had gone missing, but maybe there was a simple explanation. Maybe those people had just left. No one had to stay. It isn't as if anyone were a prisoner. At least Marisa believed that. But she had always allowed her husband to make the tough decisions. So if he thought talking to the sergeant and getting answers was the best thing to do, she'd support him, but she had a nagging suspicion things wouldn't turn out well.

"Marisa ... Earth to Marisa." Bryce waved his hands in front of her face. She shook her head to clear the fog and smiled at him. "Sorry. Just daydreaming."

He smiled and planted a kiss on her lips. "Let's go unless you're still eating."

"No, I'm finished. I'm tired, and the kids need to get to bed."

Bryce and his family headed to their room.

Paul felt eyes on him and looked up. The sergeant had been watching his table with interest. He signaled for his brother and sister to finish up and follow him out. Once in the hall, Paul breathed a little easier. The look he had seen had scared him. He thought it was a good thing that Bryce was coming with him.

Chapter 22

The knock on the door startled the sergeant. "Come in."

The door opened. Bryce and Paul walked in. The sergeant looked up from her laptop. "What can I do for you gentlemen this morning?"

"We have a few questions and concerns about the strange happenings in the hospital," Bryce said.

The sergeant stood and walked around her desk. "What questions?"

Paul took a step back toward the door. He suddenly felt like a mouse caught in a rat trap. Bryce, however, looked the sergeant straight in the eye. "First of all, we've noticed a lot of people have disappeared. Where did they go? Why's there no trespassing sign on the doors leading to the second floor? What's going on in this place? It's supposed to be a safe haven, but I'm afraid to go to sleep for fear of getting killed or suddenly go missing."

The sergeant chuckled. Nodding her head as if in time with some unheard music, she paced. She clasped her hands and tapped her lips. "Wow. You just came into my office and demanded an explanation. Who do you think you are? I'm in charge here. You don't get to come into my office and demand anything. I don't owe you any explanation. I will not answer these absurd questions. Get out!"

Paul inched closer to the door ready to flee like a scared rabbit. Bryce's face turned red. He advanced toward the sergeant. He shouted that she was not in charge and that they had every right to know what was happening in their home.

The door bursting open knocked Paul to the ground. In walked three privates. "Is everything all right in here, Sergeant?"

"Yes, Private. Bryce and Paul were just leaving."

Private Patterson put a hand on Bryce's arm. "Are you going to go quietly, or does this have to get physical?"

Bryce shook off the private's hand. "I'm going, but we're not done here. Not by a long shot. I'll find out what's going on here. I won't rest until I find out the truth." Bryce and Paul left.

"Are you sure you're okay, Sergeant?"

"I'm fine, Private. Make sure you keep an eye on those two. I don't trust that they won't try to get to the second floor."

"Understood, Sergeant."

After the privates left, the sergeant lost her composure. *That was close.* Her hand started to shake. Adrenaline was pumping through her body. Her heart was pounding so hard that she felt it would jump out of her chest. She calmed her pulse by slowing her breathing. She sat and got back to the email she had been reading. The situation in every corner of the world was getting dangerous. A solution to the outbreak needed to be found. The zombies were multiplying, and the human population was dying out.

She closed her computer. The time to strike was at hand. She needed to devise a plan before her superior showed up. He was on his way. She needed to get this place under control and erase all evidence of the metahumans. That meant everyone on the second floor would have to be disposed of. *Casualties of war.* The devious look on the sergeant's face would have given anyone nightmares.

Bryce paced in his room. "This isn't right. We have to find out what's going on. This place is more like an internment camp than a safe haven. I'm going to the second floor. Paul, are you with me, or are you going to be that coward I saw in the sergeant's office?"

Paul blanched. Bryce got in his face. "You need to grow a pair. I mean, what the hell was that performance back there?"

"Sorry, dude. Zombies I can fight, but the sergeant scares the shit out of me."

"Are you a man or a mouse?"

Marisa put her hand on Bryce's arm. "I hate to admit it, but Paul's rights. There's just something off about that woman."

Bryce looked into his wife's eyes. "Maybe so, but

something isn't right here, and I intend to get to the bottom of it. We should feel safe here. If we can't, then what do we do?"

Paul took a deep breath. "You're right. I'm with you. Let's find a way to the second floor. We need answers, and that's the only way to get them. I've been paying attention to the schedule. At midnight, they have a five-minute gap in the guards. I say we sneak onto the second floor then."

"Don't they come down the stairs?"

"No. Those idiots take the elevator and leave the door unguarded. I guess they figure everyone's asleep so they don't need to keep the door guarded then."

"Okay, we'll go at midnight."

"Tonight, bro, we get some answers."

Paul left the room. Marisa looked at her husband. Her face had turned green. "I don't like this, Bryce. What if you get caught?"

"Honey, we'll be alright. We're just going to look around and get some evidence to tell others. Then we'll have another talk with the sergeant."

"Please be careful."

Bryce kissed his wife and pulled her in for a hug. "Always, sweetheart. I promise everything will be okay."

Chapter 23

Bryce checked his watch and signaled Paul to follow him. He slowly opened the door and peeked around it. He saw the guard get on the elevator. He opened the door, and they walked through.

What he did not realize was that he had activated a silent alarm that would alert the guards if anyone entered the second floor without authorization. He did not notice the keypad on the left side of the door. The sergeant had had that installed after Tyler had found his way up to that floor.

They slowly walked down the dark hallway. They had their backs to the elevator when Private McLain got off. "Freeze! Put your hands in the air and slowly turn around."

Bryce and Paul complied. "What gives, man? We were just going to the bathroom."

"Right. And I suppose you didn't notice the no trespassing sign on the door. You tripped a silent alarm when you opened it."

Bryce put his hands down and advanced on the private.

"Stop or I'll shoot!"

"Come on, man. It was an honest mistake." Bryce continued to advance toward the private.

"I'm not kidding. If you take one more step, I'll shoot you."

"Hey, Bryce, maybe you should stop walking."

Bryce turned to Paul and winked. He took another step. The private shot him in the head.

Paul put his hands down. "What the fuck?" He walked toward Bryce's body and the private fired again, killing him.

The private dropped his rifle. "*Fuck fuck fuck!*"

"What the hell's going on?" came a voice over the walkie. "Where'd those shots come from?"

The private reached for his walkie. "We had a situation on the second floor. You need to get up here."

"On my way."

The elevator opened. Three privates and two corporals raced out. By then, the residents had come out of their rooms to see what the noise was all about. Private Patterson grabbed Private McLain's rifle just as the sergeant entered from the hallway and saw the bodies. "What the hell is going on? Be quick about it before someone else makes it to this floor. If I heard the gunfire, so did everyone else."

Private McLain said, "I was coming up on the elevator for my duty when I noticed the silent alarm had been tripped. When the door opened, I noticed these two. I told them to freeze and put their hands up. They turned around slowly. I asked them what they were doing on this floor. They said they were looking for the bathroom. I found their explanation not credible."

He pointed at Bryce's body. "He started to walk toward me. I told him to freeze or I would shoot. He didn't listen. I shot him in the head. His friend started toward the body, and I panicked. I shot him too."

"Damn it, Private! You were under strict orders not to shoot anyone! You were supposed to detain them! No one was supposed to get shot unless I gave the order and certainly not in the hospital. Are you a complete idiot?"

The private blanched at that statement.

"How were they able to get on this floor undetected?"

"Private McLain and I were switching posts," Private Patterson said. "Since it was midnight, we figured everyone was asleep. We traded places via the elevator."

Sweeping her hand over the dead men, the sergeant asked, "Does this look like everyone was asleep? And I ordered these men watched. Why weren't they being watched?"

Private Patterson said, "It was midnight, Sergeant. We felt it was okay not to have a guard since it seemed they had turned in for the night."

"Really, Private? Do I have an army of idiots working for me?"

Jessica spoke up. "Sergeant, how are you going to explain this? We told you that people were going to ask questions. You cut off the second floor and hoped no one would notice. Everyone will want some answers. How are you going to spin this?"

Rachel glared at Jessica, which made Jessica and others except the soldiers burst out laughing.

"I'll figure it out, Doctor. Thanks for the sarcasm."

"Anytime, Sergeant. I don't want to be the one to tell you I told you so, but ..." The sergeant's glare made everyone laugh again. "See ya, Sergeant. Wouldn't want to be ya." The laughter increased.

Chapter 24

The sergeant surveyed the situation. Though she hated the mega humans, Jessica was right. This mistake was not going to be easy to cover up. She looked around at her soldiers and started formulating a plan. The sergeant felt cunning enough to pull it off if she spun it just right.

She called her corporals over to the corner and told them her plan. They needed scapegoats if they were going to come out on top of this situation. Two of the privates had to be sacrificed in order for everyone else to survive. The plan was for the corporals, Private Patterson, and Private McLain to discreetly get the bodies out of the hospital a little distance away but close enough for gunshots to be heard. The corporals were to kill the privates. The story they would spin would be that the privates had acted on their own; they had gone rogue and took these men outside and killed them in cold blood. The corporals went to investigate the gunshots. They were ambushed and had no other option but to kill the privates in self-defense. One corporal needed to come back with a wound. They agreed.

This needed to be pulled off immediately. While the corporals were executing this plan, the sergeant would explain it to the other soldiers. Everyone needed to be onboard for this plan to work.

The sergeant and her corporals rejoined the group. "So we need to get these bodies outside the gate. I think Corporals Jenkins and Lemmons along with Privates Patterson and McLain should take the bodies outside the hospital. I'll come up with a credible story and have it ready to go by the time you four get back. Private Malick and Sanchez, come with me."

Private Patterson grabbed two gurneys, and they put the bodies on them. They wheeled them to the service elevator and went down to the basement and parking garage. They got them into a van and quickly left through the back exit.

Once they were outside the gates, Corporal Lemmons directed the driver to turn down a street to the right and drive about five blocks. He had Private McLain pull over and park.

Private Patterson had a funny feeling about what was happening.

The corporals got out and opened the back of the van. They removed the bodies and laid them on the ground. "Privates, get out of the van and help us."

McLain reached for the door handle, but Patterson

grabbed his arm and shook his head. McLain looked at him confused. Patterson said simply, "Drive."

McLain gave him a frown and got out of the van. Patterson quickly jumped into the driver's seat, hit the gas, and sped off. Corporal Jenkins fired his pistol into the back of the van and hit the windshield. Patterson ducked but kept driving. Jenkins raised his pistol again to fire, but the other corporal stopped him.

"What just happened?" McLain asked. "Patterson told me to drive. He acted like something bad was going to happen."

"He wasn't wrong, Private."

McLain had a surprised look on his face just before Jenkins shot him between his eyes.

"What are we going to do about that one?" Corporal Jenkins pointed toward a cloud of dust the van was kicking up as Patterson fled.

"He'll die from starvation if the zombies don't get him."

"Sounds good to me. What are we going to tell the sergeant?"

"We don't need to tell her anything. We'll just say it went off without a hitch. Oh, and one more thing." The corporal fired and winged Jenkins, who grabbed his arms as blood started to seep out.

"We're going to have to walk back. Can you walk?"

"Yes. It's just a flesh wound." Jenkins turned around and started to walk. He never saw Lemmons raise his pistol. He never saw the bullet coming. He didn't feel a thing.

Lemmons stepped over the body and walked back to the hospital. In his mind, he had done the right thing. He knew Jenkins would fail to keep his mouth shut. He began to whistle to himself as he got closer to the gate. He failed to see a woman hiding behind the building. She had seen the whole thing.

Chynna waited until the soldier was around the corner and out of sight of the main road. She knew he was a bad man and needed to be taken care of. And by the looks of him, he had plenty of meat on him. She came up behind him and quickly stabbed him with an upper thrust between the ribs and into his lung. He bled out and died in minutes. She danced around the corpse Indian style.

She heard something. She wasn't afraid of zombies. She just didn't want to share her kill. She dragged the corporal around the corner and put him in her van. She collected the other bodies as well. As she drove away, she was whistling the same tune the corporal had been whistling as she grinned just like the Cheshire Cat.

Chapter 25

Private Patterson was driving fast and paying more attention to his rearview mirror than where he was going. He looked ahead and saw cars abandoned in the middle of the street. He swerved around them but hit the curb and flipped the van on its side.

The private came to what he figured was a few hours later; the sun was much higher. He undid his seat belt and climbed through the broken windshield. He touched his forehead and came away with blood. He tore off the right arm of his uniform and pressed the fabric to his forehead. He stumbled away from the van. He knew he would need to find water and shelter soon, before it became night and the zombies became active.

He shielded his eyes from the sun and scanned the area. He came up with a plan. He headed away from the hospital toward downtown. He knew that would get him closer to the zombies, but going the other way would lead him into rural territory. He figured he had a better chance of finding food and shelter in the city.

He wanted to find a way to infiltrate the hospital and inform everyone of what had just happened but not until he had rested. He also needed to take care of his head wound before it became infected. He would try the houses along the route, but he knew they had already been ransacked by the hospital teams. He figured he would have to walk a few miles to find a viable place. He shook his head in frustration. *Dammit! How could I have been so stupid? I should have known the sergeant was up to no good. The next chance I get, I'll put a bullet in her head.*

He started to become disoriented and began to stumble. He didn't notice the caravan of army trucks coming his way. Patterson stumbled on the road. The driver of the first truck hit his horn and his brakes at the same time. Patterson collapsed and fell to his knees. The truck stopped a few inches from his head.

Private Tolliver raced out and caught Patterson before his head hit the ground. "Hey, buddy, you okay?"

"Water."

Tolliver signaled for another private to hand him a canteen. He eased Patterson down and handed him the canteen. Patterson took a long drink. "Thanks."

"What are you doing out here? It's dangerous."

"Long story."

A shadow fell over the privates. "Well, son, it's a story I'd like to hear."

Patterson blinked a couple of times before he realized who was talking. He tried to get up but got dizzy.

"Easy, son. Take your time."

Patterson got to his feet and as best he could saluted General Anthony Staley, who looked at the private and chuckled before returning the salute. "Join me in the van and tell me your story. The sun's going down. I can hear zombies moving around."

A few zombies wandered from around the corners of some houses. The privates opened fire and killed all five zombies. Patterson put his hands up in an attempt to get them to stop. "No more! We need to leave this area before you kill any more humans."

"Humans?" the general asked.

"Part of my story."

The general gestured toward the van, and Patterson got in. The caravan started to move, and the private started telling his story. The general showed no emotion as the story unfolded. They arrived at the hospital gates just as the private finished his story.

"Looks like I have some facts to corroborate. Mega humans, living zombies, and unauthorized killings. That's a lot of information to take in. Are you ready for this, soldier?"

"Yes sir. This issue needs to be solved."

"Here's your chance."

The gates opened. The caravan entered. They pulled up in front of the hospital. Sergeant Johanson and Privates Malick and Sanchez were out front to greet them. The general got out first.

The sergeant saluted. "Sir, good to see you again."

"Sergeant, I've heard some disturbing news."

"Disturbing news, sir? From whom did you hear it, sir?"

"From me, Sergeant," Private Patterson said as he exited the van.

A shocked look flashed across the sergeant's and the privates' faces and quickly disappeared, but the damage had been done; the general had caught it. "Sergeant, you have some explaining to do to me and the people in there," he said as he pointed at the faces peering out of the hospital windows.

The sergeant turned and saw a crowd gathering around the doors. Sweat formed on her upper lip. She quickly licked it off before turning to the general. His smile told her she was in so much trouble. He gestured toward the doors. "Shall we?"

The sergeant nodded. "Of course, sir. After you."

"No, Sergeant, you go first."

The sergeant smiled politely and nodded. She straightened her uniform and started walking toward the entrance. The electronic doors opened and the sergeant and the others entered. Those gathered at the door stepped aside to let them in.

Just as the doors closed, Marisa walked up to the sergeant and slapped her face. "Where's my husband? Don't give me that crap you tried to spin this morning about Bryce and Paul going out to help with zombie captures! I don't believe it! Paul's family isn't buying it either. What were those gunshots we all heard this morning? Don't try to sell me on the private getting spooked and firing into the wall. I want answers! We all do!"

"Sergeant," the general asked, "do you have an explanation for these people?" When the sergeant could only stammer, he said, "Let me help you." He turned to Marisa. "On behalf of the United States Army, I express my condolences for your loss. Your husband was killed along with his friend Paul."

Marisa's hands flew to her face. Her tears began to fall. Paul's sister gulped and fought the urge to cry. She asked what was on everyone's minds. "How? Why?"

"I can answer that," Patterson said. Everyone turned to him. "They were on the second floor, where they were not authorized to be. Private McLain discovered them. According to McLain, Bryce kept advancing on him. He panicked and shot Bryce and then Paul even though he was under orders not to shoot anyone.

"The sergeant wanted to cover up the debacle. She and the corporals came up with a plan. They were supposed to take us outside the hospital and kill McLain and me. I'm not sure what their story will be, only that I was supposed to die."

Marisa lunged at the sergeant, but she sidestepped Marisa, who collapsed in a crying rage. Paul's brother and sister surround Marisa; they grieved their loss.

"Sergeant, show me what's on the second floor." He addressed the crowd. "Once I find out what has happened and is happening here, you'll be informed I promise. I know you don't have much faith in the army right now, but I assure you no more lies. Let's go, Sergeant." They went up to the second floor.

Thomas was bouncing Trisha in his arms when the sergeant got off the elevator. "Hello, Sergeant. Anything I can do for you?"

The general, right behind the sergeant, stared at Trisha. She looked at him and smiled. "Daddy! Down please!" Thomas obliged his daughter, who walked over to the general. He bent over, and she stuck out her hand for a shake. He took her tiny hand in his and smiled. "Well, hello little lady. How old are you?"

"I'm seven months old."

The general looked up in surprise.

"Trisha is what we call a mega human. She contracted the zombie virus while in the womb. She was given a series of different oxygen doses during her transformation."

"This is fascinating … uh …"

"Dr. Thomas Matthews. The young lady is my daughter, Trisha."

The general looked from Thomas to Trisha. "You seem quite human."

"I am."

"My daughter and my wife are what we're calling mega humans. I'm an ordinary human. There are only five mega humans on this floor and possibly in the world. They all received oxygen therapy within minutes of contact with zombies. Within a month, they were fully transformed."

"Fascinating. What's the difference between them and normal humans?"

"They learn very quickly, and they have one red eye. I'm not sure about the purpose for that. Could be just a side effect of the virus. They have two hearts, and their lungs are bigger. I'm not sure if you're aware, General, but the atmosphere has changed. There is more oxygen in the air that in the long run will ultimately kill off humans like us."

"I see. And Trisha is able to communicate at only seven months?"

"Yes. My working theory is that one month for her is like a year for us. Or at least her learning capacity has increased at that general rate."

"Sounds logical."

The sergeant was looking on in horror at the exchange. *No way this is logical! None of this makes any sense. I need to end this now starting with this devil child!* She snatched a gun from a private and pointed it at Trisha.

"Sergeant Johanson! Put down that weapon!" the general barked.

"No! This isn't right. She shouldn't even exist! Can't you all see that? This child is an abomination, and you're all being brainwashed! I'm going to end this before more of them exist!"

The sergeant's hands were shaking. The general moved between the sergeant and the child.

"Step away from the child, General. I don't want to shoot you."

"Then put down the gun, Sergeant."

"I can't. I have to save the human race!"

"The human race as we know it is dead. She and others of her kind are the future of the human race."

"General, they have you brainwashed. Where's the proof the atmosphere has changed and will ultimately poison the human race?" She was having trouble focusing on the people in front of her, and she started to hear a ringing in her ears.

Thomas started to advance toward her, and she swung the gun toward him. "Don't move!"

Thomas threw up his hands as if to say *Whoa!* and backed up. "Are you okay, Sergeant? You seem a little on edge."

The sergeant blinked. "I can't see. I can't breathe. And my ears are ringing."

"The effects of atmospheric change. They're starting to affect all of us. If a cure for this isn't found, those of us who haven't morphed will eventually become delusional and our organs will shut down. We will die of asphyxiation not from a lack of oxygen but from too much of it."

The sergeant's hands began to shake harder. She didn't hear someone come up behind her. An arm snaked around her throat and put her in a choke hold. Jessica whispered into the sergeant's ear, "I told you I'd kill you if you threatened my child. Now you get to witness my rage."

The sergeant struggled with Jessica and managed to

back her against the wall causing Jessica to loosen her grip. She turned around, and Jessica's backhand spun her around and knocked the sergeant about five feet down the hall. The gun dropped out of the sergeant's hand, and she crawled on all fours for it. Jessica was upon her before she got to it, and they wrestled for the gun. Jessica threw her against the wall with such force that the back of the sergeant's head exploded and splattered the wall with blood and brains. Jessica got up and with the pistol in hand walked to the sergeant to kick her just to make sure she was dead. Anyone seeing the red splatter and gray brain matter on the wall knew the sergeant was dead. The general with Trisha in his arms surveyed the damage.

"I call that self-defense. How about the rest of you?"

All the soldiers nodded.

The general turned to Thomas. "How about you show me the rest of these facilities."

Thomas stepped around the sergeant's body. "Right this way, General."

Chapter 26

The general straightened his uniform and addressed those in front of him. "Are you ready to tell the world about the megahumans?"

"Can we just start with the people in this hospital first?" Tyler asked, and the general laughed at the statement especially as a ten-year-old megahuman had asked it.

"I'm serious, General," Tyler said. "We need to see how the ones we live with will react first."

"Okay," the general said. "We'll take the elevator down, and I'll get off first. Everyone should be gathered in the hospital lobby. For those not able to leave their rooms, we have monitors set up for the unveiling."

"We're not a circus act, you know."

"I know, Tyler. It's just that this has to be done correctly. We don't want a reaction like the one we got from the sergeant. I need to handle this with a delicate touch. Especially Trisha. She's bound to get quite a reaction. She's eight months going on eight years, you know. I want the megahumans to be the last to get out of the elevator and stay behind the others until I'm ready to introduce you. Everyone clear on that?"

Those gathered around him nodded. Everyone got on the elevator in the correct order. As the door closed, the general's eyes were slightly yellow with a touch of purple, a sign that a change was beginning to occur in him.

The elevator door opened. Everyone filed out into the corridor.

Marisa asked, "What's this all about, General?. You told us there'd be no more lies and yet we haven't heard anything from you in weeks."

"I know it's been longer than I expected, but I had to get all the answers before I could tell you the truth. May 25, 2025, marked the beginning or, as some thought, the end of the world as we knew it. I can now say without a doubt that the world has changed and we must adapt or die."

The crowd gasped. "What do you mean, General?"

"I'm going to introduce you to some people who have been living on the second floor. But before I do, I need you to understand that what I'm about to show you is no cause for alarm. When the black rain fell, some people contracted a virus changing normal people into zombies. Those who received oxygen within minutes became something else. Before I introduce these extraordinary humans to you, I need to explain a few things. The atmosphere changed during the rain, which caused the oxygen level to rise. Because of this, human beings in their present state will eventually die from too much oxygen. However, if we adapt, we will survive."

"How do we adapt, General?"

"The human body is remarkable. We have scientists working on an antidote that will change the human body in ways that will allow us to thrive in this new environment. Right now, the only way to adapt causes humans to go through a metamorphosis that takes a month and large doses of oxygen. During this time, these humans grow an extra heart, and the lungs expand and grow for the intake of extra oxygen."

He had everyone's attention.

"What's your proof for this theory, General?"

"It's not a theory, Marisa. It's a fact. What I'm about to show you is actual data taken from these megahumans. Once you've seen this footage, you'll understand. I'll then introduce you to the actual megahumans."

The general hit a play button, and screens descended from the ceiling. A video showed megahumans and their abilities as well as x-rays of their organs. Everyone watched in shocked silence. When the video ended and the screens ascended, everyone turned to the general, who simply stepped aside as Jessica and the others came forward. The silence in the room was deafening.

"Hi, everyone," Trisha said.

"Hold on!" someone said. "Did you just say hi?"

"Yes," a giggling Trisha said.

The general walked to the podium among loud murmuring. "People, settle down."

Jessica took over. "Let me explain. I was infected while pregnant with this beautiful, sweet girl. She was born infected and was transformed shortly after she was born. Her learning capacity increased exponentially, about a year every month. She has all the capacities of an eight-year-old and more though she's only eight months old. We're harmless, but we are the next evolution of humankind. We are smarter, stronger, and quicker than you are, and we can breathe in this atmosphere, which is slowly poisoning all of you. Have any of you felt light-headed? Have trouble seeing? Are your hands shaking? Are your eyes turning yellow with a hint of purple?"

Everyone was in shock. "What do we do? How long do we have?" someone asked.

"We're not sure. We have scientists working on the issue. We're trying to find an antidote that can transform all of you into us."

"Why can't we just transform as you did?"

"Despite the fact that we have enough beds, we don't have enough of the oxygen you'd need to transform as we did."

The general spoke over the murmuring crowd. "People, please. We're working as fast as we can to fix this problem. Please bear with us. We might need your help."

"Whatever you need! We're more than willing to help."

"For now, just remain calm. All of you need to be checked out by the doctors. Find the room bearing the initial of your last name and form a line in front of it."

The crowd dispersed to find their correct rooms. Jessica and Thomas headed to the exam rooms to help. The general turned to the rest of the group. "Well, that went smoothly."

"Okay. Can I go play now? I'm bored."

Trisha's question made everyone laugh.

Chapter 27

D ana was quietly watching her father and the other scientist working. Every time they thought there was a breakthrough, they had a major setback. She was hoping they would notice what they hadn't included in the mix, one key ingredient—human blood.

They had been changing the quantities of megahuman blood and trying to mix it with zombie blood. It has been eight months since this collaboration had begun, but they were no closer to finding the cure.

Dana had been repeatedly running an algorithm on her computer, and it had finally come back with a viable combination the previous night. She needed to tell her father. It wasn't that he didn't believe she was smart; it was just that he was an arrogant scientist. She loved her father very much, but he had a way of dismissing her ideas just because she didn't have a degree.

Jonathan paced the floor and looked at yet another dead zombie on a slab. He knew there were five more zombies in the morgue, but he couldn't keep using them as lab rats. They were humans after all.

The door opened. In walked Thomas and the general, who looked at the damage on the walls caused by the glass slides the frustrated scientists had thrown at them one failure after another.

"So I see we still have no answers," the general said. He bent over and coughed hard. He stood erect and took a deep breath. "It's getting harder to breathe. Feels like my insides are burning up."

"Yeah, that seems about right, but to state the obvious, no, we just killed another one."

Dana cleared her throat to get everyone's attention. Jonathan looked at her in frustration. "What?"

Dana gave him a nasty look. She narrowed her eyes and pursed her lips. Jonathan did exactly the same. "Well, are you going to say something or just stand there giving me your death stare?"

Dana unfolded her arms and relaxed. "Look. I know I don't have a degree, but all these months, I've watched you trying different combinations and killing zombies. You forgot to add one ingredient." She paused.

Thomas gave her a quizzical look. "Don't keep us waiting."

"I've been running an algorithm on my computer. Last night, it came back with 99.9 percent probability that the antidote requires a combination of blood from the megahumans, zombies, and humans. According to my research, the correct combination is 33 percent of the first two and 34 percent of the last."

Jonathan pondered that for a minute before he began to assemble that combination. He placed a drop of this concoction on a slide, put it under the microscope, and peered through the eyepiece. "Hmmm. Interesting. That combination seems to be working. Before, the megahuman and zombie blood simply canceled each other out, but with the introduction of human blood, it's sustaining and is a red coagulant. This might work. We need another zombie."

"Not a problem," the general said. He got on his walkie and instructed his soldiers to bring another zombie from the morgue. Within minutes, a zombie body was there. Jonathan filled a syringe a third full with the combination. He looked at his daughter. "Does your algorithm say how much to give them?"

"No, but I'd start with a third."

"Great minds think alike." He smiled at his daughter. He swabbed a clean spot on the zombie's arm and injected the serum. The zombie suddenly went into convulsions, but within minutes, it stopped thrashing around and started actually breathing. The color began to return to her face. Jonathan touched the zombie and realized her body temperature was rising. He listened to her heart with a stethoscope; it was beating normally. He checked the other side and realized the zombie had two hearts. "I can't call her a zombie anymore. She's become a megahuman."

Chapter 28

"What do you mean she's a megahuman?" Thomas looked at the doctor who was perplexed by his statement. "I mean exactly that. She has two hearts, and her lung capacity is most likely increased."

"Incredible." The general rubbed his callused hands in anticipation. "Will this work on humans who need to be turned into megahumans as well?"

While Jonathan contemplated the question, Dana checked her laptop's calculations. "According to my algorithm, the probability is about 95 percent. We'd need a test subject to—"

Before she finished that statement, Thomas had filled a syringe with the blood and injected himself. Jessica walked in just as Thomas was doing that. "What the hell have you done?" She ran to his side just as he collapsed to the floor in convulsions. The convulsions were violent—Thomas thrashed around on the floor like a beached whale—but they lasted just a minute. Once the convulsions ceased, he began to breathe normally. He opened his eyes. Jessica saw that one had turned red just like all the megahumans. When he smiled, she punched him in the chest. "You bloody idiot! What would have happened had the injection made you a zombie or killed you?"

"Somebody had to be the guinea pig. I figured I might as well be."

The new megahuman on the table began to stir. "What happened? Where am I?" Thomas got up. Jonathan grabbed a stethoscope and examined the girl. "Can you tell me your name?"

"Yeah … Umm … Uh … Marie. Marie Baumgard. And my head hurts."

"Do you remember what happened to you?"

"Uh … Umm … Yeah, I think. The last thing I remember is trying to hide in an abandoned warehouse, but there were zombies there."

"You were bitten. You transformed into a zombie. We're not sure how long you were in this zombie state. It took us eight months to find a cure."

"I was a zombie? So I was dead? How do you cure the dead?"

"No, not dead. You still had a heartbeat and brain function. They were just a lot slower. You were trying to take care of your primal needs. As a zombie, you probably attacked people and consumed some flesh."

"*Ewww!* I'm a vegetarian!" She shrunk back in horror.

Jessica approached Marie. "I don't mean to be rude, but you haven't bathed in a very long time. You stink."

"Is that me? Wow. Do you have a place for me to clean up?"

"Yes. Right this way. Once we've cleaned you up, I'll do a thorough exam."

The two headed for the showers.

Jonathan looked at the remaining antidote. "We'll need an exact count of the people in the hospital. Do we have enough human blood to create this antidote? I'm not sure if our blood in this present state can be used to create it."

"I hope so. We have some in store on the third floor. We got our monthly supply a day before all hell broke loose."

The general's walkie crackled with static; a voice came through. "General, we have a problem. The zombies have surrounded the hospital. They're awake in the middle of the day. That's weird in itself, but weirder is that they aren't trying to tear down the wall. They just seem to be in a trance."

Anthony grabbed his walkie off his belt. "How many?"

"About a dozen, but more keep coming. Oh shit. They're advancing toward the south gate. What do we do? With this many, they could easily breach the fence."

Anthony looked at the doctors. "Do we have enough antidote to try to cure these people?"

"That'll take some time to create. Plus, we need to make sure everyone in the hospital gets this cure first."

The voice crackled over the walkie. "General, we need orders, sir. All of a sudden they are trying to get in. What do we do?"

"Do what you have to do, Private. The safety of the people in this hospital is necessary."

"We're going to need backup."

"Copy that. We're on our way." He looked at the three scientists. "You stay here. Get the antidote ready. Thomas, I need you and anyone else who can handle a weapon. I have to make a decision. I realize killing them means we're killing humans, but we need to survive. The needs of the many outweigh the needs of the few if humanity's going to survive, and we need to act quickly before more come."

The general and Thomas ran out of the lab.

"Looks like it's up to us to save what's left of the human race. Roll up your sleeves and get to work."

The laboring scientists heard gunshots as they scrambled to create a life-saving antidote. Hope and despair pervaded their reality. *What if there isn't enough? What happens to those we can't save? Who makes that decision?* But they had no time to answer such questions, including *How the hell can we vaccinate every zombie without getting killed ourselves?*

Chapter 29

Thomas raced into the morgue, where the scientists were preparing the antidote. Dr. Foster and Dana stared at him in confusion. "You have enough of the antidote ready to give to everyone in the hospital?"

Dr. Foster peeled off his latex gloves and pitched them into the waste receptacle. "Yes, we have enough for everyone in the hospital, but why were you running?"

"Every time you cure a zombie, we get attacked. I hate having to kill them, but we have to survive."

"Good news. We have just one more zombie to cure. He's being brought up now."

The door opened. Luke wheeled in a subdued zombie on a gurney. Thomas got on his walkie and informed the soldiers outside to be prepared for one more attack.

Dana filled a syringe with the antidote and approached the zombie. "Here we go." She injected the zombie and stepped back, waiting for the antidote to kick in. A few minutes passed. Nothing happened. "What's going on?"

"Don't know. It should have worked by now."

"Can we give him another injection?"

"We can try." Dana grabbed another syringe of the antidote and injected the zombie. Still no response. "Someone give me an empty syringe so I can draw blood."

Jonathan handed his daughter a syringe. She drew blood, squirted some on a plate, put it under the microscope, and looked hard. The zombie began to thrash around. "Here we go—delayed reaction!"

But the zombie stopped convulsing. Blood or something that looked like it began running out of his ears, nose, and mouth. It was black as oil. "What the hell?" Luke looked puzzled.

Dana and Jonathan approached the zombie; Jonathan checked the zombie's vitals with his stethoscope. "He's dead."

"What do you mean dead?"

"He's not breathing."

"Maybe a reaction to the antidote."

"How'd that happen?"

Dana went back to the microscope. "This would explain why his blood is black rather than dark red."

"What?"

"Take a look."

Thomas, Jonathan, and Luke did.

"What does this mean?"

"Let's look at what we know," Dana said. "One, zombies are living, breathing creatures that have mutated. Two, megahuman blood kills them. Three, their blood is usually a deep dark-red but never black. So what's the difference between this zombie and the others?"

Jonathan rubbed his chin. "For one, the blood is black—oil-slick black. An autopsy is necessary. We need to check all the organs and stomach contents. We need another zombie. One just killed trying to get into the compound will do. I don't want to kill one unless it's necessary."

Thomas and Luke headed out to grab a zombie corpse and shortly came back with one on a gurney. Dana looked it over. "The one difference I can see is that the blood has its usual red look." The guys looked from one zombie to the next and concurred. "So the next thing we need to do is to conduct autopsies."

"Not a problem. It's the one thing all doctors have to do whether they're scientists or medical doctors. Thomas and Luke, work on the zombie you brought in. Dana and I will work on this one. We need to record and photograph the autopsies," Jonathan said.

"So we need a couple of cameras."

"Or we could just use our smartphones and take some video," Dana said. "I mean, come on! Who has cameras these days?"

Luke rolled his eyes. "Teenagers."

Dana put her hands on her hips. "Who are you calling a teenager? I graduated at age fifteen from high school, and I was about to graduate from college with a bachelor's in science in a couple of months when this chaos happened. I may be only twenty, but I'm far from being a teenager."

Luke held up his hands in mock defeat. "I stand corrected." Everyone laughed. "Let's get to work."

With Thomas and Luke on one side and Jonathan and Dana on another, they started in on their respective zombies. They recorded and weighed all the organs. They examined the stomach contents and drew several vials of blood. They cut open the crania and autopsied the brains to check for differences. Once all the info was gathered, they came together to compare notes.

"Seems everything's the same except the stomach contents. Our zombie seems to have digested fruits, vegetables, and what appears to be animal meat."

"Our zombie is similar, except this piece of somewhat digested meat seems to be human in origin. That might account for the antidote not working."

Dana had been analyzing the blood. "I agree with that. The blood on the right is the blood from our zombie. The blood on the left is the blood from the other. From what I can deduce, the blood from our zombie is black because it had absorbed the blood from the human flesh and received more enzymes, which made the antidote null and void."

"Why do they have the extra enzymes? I mean, if they're human, why didn't the body absorb the extra enzymes?"

"If I had to guess," Dana said, "I'd say it's because they have a slower metabolism, the extra intake in human enzymes could not be absorbed into the bloodstream, and that caused a backup in the body."

"So do we try to create another antidote?" Luke looked at both Dana and Thomas for an answer.

Dana answered without hesitation. "I don't think we have time. We have to design a way to deliver the antidote we have to the ones we can save and, as much as I hate to say it, sacrifice those we can't. I mean, saving the human race doesn't come without sacrifices."

Thomas shook his head in agreement "I hate to say it, but I agree. This means some of the people out there won't get their families back. That is going to be a hard pill to swallow. Right now, we need a way to inject the zombies and save the world."

"I can help you with that."

Everyone looked toward the door and saw Private Patterson.

"What can we do for you, Private Patterson?"

"It's Ben. Sorry to interrupt. I just thought I needed to tell you my idea."

"Let's have it," Thomas said as he leaned against the table and crossed his arms. He realized Patterson felt threatened by that gesture, so he uncrossed his arms.

"I have a way to administer the antidote. People have been finding ways of committing murder without leaving evidence. Ice bullets, for instance. My idea is to create ice bullets using the antidote."

Dana said, "The zombies have a body temperature

lower than a normal human's. How's the bullet supposed to melt and allow the antidote to enter the bloodstream?"

Patterson continued with his explanation. "The bullet should shatter on impact and release the antidote."

Dana pursued her lips before answering "Sounds plausible, but we don't have enough people who know how to shoot."

Patterson answered her "Aren't you about to administer the antidote to everyone? Changing them into megahumans? One of the perks of this, and correct me if I'm wrong, is heightened intelligence and the ability to learn new things quickly."

Thomas interjects "You're right. And we know megahuman blood is toxic to the zombies. So if we get bitten, they die."

"Okay, so we need to administer the antidote to all humans and ask for volunteers and train them."

"One problem, boys," Dana said. "We made only enough antidote for the people in the hospital. It would take at least another week to make more, and we need more blood."

"So before we administer the antidote to everyone in the hospital, we need them to donate blood. Will that be enough to create what we need?" Asks Luke

"Yeah." Dana says

"So we need to get the blood, and then we need to freeze it into bullets. We also need to train every volunteer to shoot. Do we have enough rifles?" Asks Thomas looking at Patterson.

Patterson smiled. "The caravan that arrived with the general was loaded with weapons, including scoped rifles. That should be adequate enough to deliver the antidote."

"We have one more problem. I heard this antidote doesn't work on zombies who have consumed human flesh. We'll also need regular bullets because if they're immune to the antidote, we'll need to kill them. I know they won't be any harm to any of us, but it needs to be taken care of."

"Boys, there's one more problem we haven't considered. How do we keep the bullets from melting?"

"Thought of that. Doesn't the hospital have those chests that transport organs in and dry ice for that purpose? We pack the bullets in one of those chests and surround them with dry ice. I'm thinking one chest for each team of two."

"Sounds like a plan."

Thomas, Luke, and Ben headed out the door to inform the people of the issue at hand. Dana and Jonathan started gathering equipment to draw blood. Once the blood was drawn, they would then give each person the antidote. It would be a long day.

Chapter 30

"Today's going to be the turning point," the general announced. "We're going out there to save a town, but in reality, we'll be saving humanity. I'm proud to be a part of this new life. We'll redefine what humankind is after today. We've been given the gift of life and a clear and longer path that doesn't lead to self-destruction. Let's go save the world."

Everyone clapped and whistled at the general's statement.

"Thank you. Those who volunteered and have learned to shoot, please gather your supplies and meet the soldiers at the door to receive your assignments. Those of you who are willing to drive the vans, please report to the garage for your assignments. Good luck everyone, and remember you need to change to regular bullets and fire into the head if a zombie fails to turn. Some loved ones will be killed, but that's very unfortunate.

"If you come face-to-face with a loved one who cannot be saved, shoot. Do not hesitate. You'd do them a disservice if you let them die that way. Peace is the best gift you can give them. Remember who they were, not what they've become."

Thomas took a deep breath as he was about to report to the soldiers in front. Jessica said, "Hey, my hero, you know how much I love you. And please don't get shot in the head. If you don't come back to me, I'll kill you."

Thomas laughed and kissed her. They headed to their assignments.

"Hey, Thomas, did you really think you'd get a different partner?"

"Luke, my man. So are you saying I'm stuck with you?"

"Yeah, looks that way."

They grabbed their gear and headed to the army van. Their team consisted of two shooters and one driver. Just as they reached the jeep, Ben joined them. "Hey, guys, looks like we're going to be hanging together."

They load the equipment into the van, and Luke takes the wheel. They drove through the gate and turned south toward the center of town. A van followed behind with Jessica at the wheel and Jesse beside her.

"So we just load up and follow this path. Shoot any zombie we see and allow for our companions to grab them once they've turned."

"Yeah, they'll be following the same path."

"Heads up. Here come the first ones."

Thomas and Ben quickly loaded their rifles and fired. The zombies fell, and within a matter of minutes, they began to turn. One was convulsing like the last one in the morgue. Thomas realized no real bullets were needed; the zombies who did not change died instantly—the antidote either changed them or killed them.

He got on his walkie and informed everyone. "Why didn't that cross my mind before? The zombie in the morgue died after we gave him two shots. What if he was already dying from the first one? I just assumed we'd overloaded his system and he crashed. All we have to do now is to shoot them and they'll simply die. That makes it easier to load and fire."

The walkie crackled. The general said, "Good observation, Thomas. Does everyone copy?"

The walkie crackled as each team acknowledged that.

A voice came over the walkie. "We need help! We're being pinned down on Stanton Street. We're being shot at. I know we're megahumans, but even we won't come back from a head shot."

Thomas grabbed his walkie. "Who's shooting at you and from where?"

"Don't know. We're pinned behind the van. Every time one of us pokes his head up, shots are fired. Pete got shot in the arm. The bleeding is under control. He was lucky. But we need backup. We hear zombies. I know that if they bite us, they die, but what happens if we get attacked by too many? Is it possible to die from being torn apart?"

"Duh! Hold on, Shawn. Try to get back in the van and hide. We're on our way."

They heard a voice in the distance. "You need to get

off my land and stop shooting at people. They have a right to live just like we do!"

Shawn said, "We know. We're shooting them with a vaccine. We're saving them."

"So why are you shooting them?"

"It's the only way to deliver the vaccine. It's an ice bullet that shatters on impact. The antidote mixes in their bloodstream and changes them."

"I don't believe you. Get the hell off my property. I won't allow you to harm my family. If you stay, I'll kill you!"

"Hey, Shawn," came a voice over the walkie. "We're on the other side of the house. We came around back. We're going to try to sneak up behind and get the shooter to stop."

The van doors flew open, and Shawn and Pete were blinded by a flashlight shining in their eyes. "I told you I'd kill you if you didn't leave."

Chynna leveled her gun but felt the cold steel of a rifle poking her back. "I don't think you want to do that. I'm not going to hurt you. Drop the rifle and put your hands behind your back. We'll walk with you back to your house and explain the situation. Shawn, get Pete to the hospital."

Pete removed his bandage. "I'm okay. The wound has almost healed. I guess we heal quickly too."

"Can your group continue on your mission? We'll deal with this."

Shawn and Pete drove off with their group.

"Okay, lady, let's go."

Thomas, Luke, and the others went inside Chynna's house.

Chapter 31

"Let me go!" Chynna yelled as she struggled against her handcuffs.

"Not until you listen to what I have to say," Thomas said.

Chynna spat in his face. "I don't need to listen to jack shit."

Ben advanced toward her until Thomas held up his hand to stop him. He stared at Chynna. "What's your name?"

"Chynna. And you're trespassing and holding me against my will. This is kidnapping! I demand you let me go and get off my property before I put a bullet the size of Manhattan in your ass!"

"Chynna. May I call you Chynna?"

"It's my name, dumbass!"

"Okay, Chynna. My name's Thomas. I'm a doctor from the hospital. Scientists and doctors there have been working on a cure for the zombie virus for months. We finally have one. I don't know if you've noticed, but it's been getting harder to breathe because humans can't handle these increased oxygen levels. Our cure changes zombies and humans into megahumans, people with larger lungs and two hearts. The transformation takes a few minutes, and the metamorphosis hurts for a second. But then, life becomes different and you get a new lease on life. How does that sound?"

"I'm educated. I served in the military. Why are you talking to me like I'm a two-year-old? You can use big words."

"Sorry, Chynna. I meant no disrespect."

"So you're saying there's a cure and my family will return to normal?"

"Well, not exactly normal."

"Yeah—megahumans, whatever. But there's a cure?"

"Yes. Where's your family?"

"In the shed out back. I have them locked in there for their safety."

"Let's give them the antidote. Would you like to go first?"

"Not until my family's been cured. Could you please uncuff me?"

Thomas released Chynna, who rubbed her wrists. She led them out and said, "If my family dies, you'll join them. I was paying attention about your buddy healing quickly. So I'll make the shot clean, quick, and in the head. Megahumans, zombies, or regular humans, you'll be dead."

Ben gave Thomas and Luke a look that said, *This bitch is crazy.* Thomas and Luke nodded at that.

Chynna approached the shed and unlocked it. She reached in and turned on the light.

Ben said, "We need you to back up. Luke, Thomas, let's line up and all fire at once."

They were aiming at the three in the shed when a zombie came over the hill. Without thinking, Luke shot the zombie in the leg. The zombie continued to approach for a few seconds before falling and going into convulsions. Within minutes, the zombie regained color and could move. She sat up and blinked.

"Okay, I believe you," Chynna said. "I was about to put a bullet in each of your heads, but after seeing that, I'll leave your brains intact."

Luke reloaded, and Chynna put her gun down. They shot the three zombies in their arms, and the zombies began to convulse. Thomas, Luke, and Ben walked toward the van.

"Where are you going?" Chynna asked.

"We need to reload our rifles in case another zombie makes it over the hill."

In reality, they wanted to make sure they had cover just in case the bullets killed the zombies. They made it to the jeep just as Chynna screamed.

"Oh shit! Duck!" They hid behind the jeep just as shots were fired.

"What the hell! You killed my family!" Chynna screamed.

"Did you feed your family human flesh?"

"Yeah. So what?"

"Feeding them flesh condemned them to death. Eating human flesh makes the vaccine ineffective."

Shots rang out again. "You left that part out!"

"I know. I'm sorry. We had to deliver the vaccine. Either way, we saved them."

"Saved them? Are you as dumb as you look? My family's dead! I'll never get to hold my children again or make love to my husband. You ruined my life! I'm going to end yours."

"Chynna, listen! They wouldn't have had any life as they were. Those things you just said about your family wouldn't have been possible if they had stayed like that. Now you can give them a decent burial and get on with your life."

"My life? You gotta be kidding me! You destroyed my life!"

Chynna shot the new megahuman in the brain, instantly killing her. "If my family can't live in this new world, neither can anyone else!"

Thomas saw the girl fall. "Chynna, that wasn't necessary."

"The hell it wasn't! You should have continued to find a way to save the ones who ate human flesh."

"There wasn't time. And we were running out of resources. The decision had to be made. The needs of the many outweigh the needs of the few."

"Are you fuckin' kidding me? You dare quote Spock to me? You really are a dumbass!"

Chynna came around the van and raised her gun to fire. A hole opened in her head and blood splattered on them. Thomas stood and looked at the general standing there with a smoking gun. "Why did you do that? We could have reasoned with her!"

"Really, Thomas? From what I heard, your skills were lacking."

Thomas was about to say something else when he felt a hand on his arm. He looked behind and saw Jessica. "He's right, sweetheart. She was going to kill you. This change of events sent her over the edge. The loss of her family was too much for her to bear. She killed an innocent. She would have just kept going and would have been a real threat to humankind. Who knows how many us she would have taken down before we took her out? A preemptive strike was needed."

"I suppose you're right."

"We have work to do. We have to save the world." Jessica smiled at him. He smiled back. Together, they set off to save the world.

EPILOGUE

S ammy looked up from the rocking chair. She closed the notebook she had been writing in and reached down to pet the small dog at her feet. She looked out the window and saw a red Camaro coming and raising a cloud of dust as it did. The last of the group had arrived.

Sammy looked up at the bright-blue sky. Five years had passed since the end of the zombie virus. Everyone was moving past it, and life had returned to normal—or the new normal, as it was called.

She and Lucy had just turned nineteen. School had become a thing of the past. Megahumans who wanted to learn something simply picked up a book and absorbed the information. Then, mentors helped them complete their education and training in any field. They had to make sure there was a need for whatever field they chose.

For the most part, people learned how to create better ways to advance electronics or grow enough food to feed the world. Although they were genetically enhanced humans, there was still the issue of hunger.

However, it seemed that there was a need to explore other planets. The world was not void of issues. The justice system still needed to be put back in place. People were still trying to get rich and rule the world. Go figure. Was humanity still on a path to self-destruction, or was it on the verge of self-discovery?

The Camaro pulled into the drive and stopped. Four people emerged. "Hey, Sammy."

"Hey, Thomas, Jessica, Tyler, and Trisha."

Trisha turned at the mention of her name. "Hi, Sammy. The food smells delicious."

"Thanks. That's meat from my farm."

"How's it going with your new superfeed?"

"Great. The modifications I've introduced seem to create more meat. My next endeavor, as you can see, is wheat."

Thomas looked at the wheat field. "Wow. How high is the wheat? I'd say about as tall as Tyler here, five-eight?"

"That's about right."

Lucy opened the door and poked her head out. "Hey, guys, are you going to keep yapping, or are you going to join us in the backyard?"

They followed Lucy through the house and into the backyard. Luke handed Thomas a beer, which Thomas sipped and said, "Man, this is awesome!"

"Thank you. It took me six months to perfect it."

"Bravo," Jessie said, coming up next to Luke.

Jessica gave her a hug. "Well look at you. You're glowing!"

"Yes, I am. Pregnancy suits me. I'm glad you're my doctor."

"These days, that's all I can do. Oh, and treat the elderly. Has anyone invented a youth serum yet?"

"No, but I hear someone from Spain is working on one."

Sammy raised her glass. "A toast to humankind. We've finally been given the wisdom to go beyond our self-destructive nature and usher humankind into a new age."

"I'll drink to that," Tyler said.

"That had better be soda or apple juice, young man."

"Come on, Mom. I'm fifteen now!"

"And that means what to me? The drinking age is still twenty-one, mister."

Thomas leaned over and whispered in Tyler's ear, "I wouldn't argue with her, son."

"Yeah, I know. Five years and you'd think I'd have learned that."

Everyone smiled. Jessica looked at her daughter, who seemed to be deep in thought. "What's wrong, honey?"

"I was just thinking about Sammy's toast. I was wondering if we really were given a chance to save humankind or if we've been handed the ability to destroy ourselves sooner."

Everyone turned to look at the five-year-old.

Printed in the United States
by Baker & Taylor Publisher Services